BLACKMAILING BENJAMIN
A REBEL LUST TABOO NOVELLA

OPHELIA BELL

ANIMUS PRESS

All rights reserved. No part of this book may be reproduced in any form or by any electronic means, including information storage and retrieval systems, without permission in writing from the author, except by a reviewer who may quote brief passages in review.

This is a work of fiction. Names, places, characters, and events are fictitious in every regard. Any similarities to actual events and persons, living or dead, is purely coincidental. Any trademarks, service marks, product names, or named features are assumed to be the property of their respective owners, and are used only for reference. There is no implied endorsement if any of these terms are used.

Blackmailing Benjamin

Copyright © 2014 Ophelia Bell

Cover Art Designed by Opulent Swag and Designs

Photograph Copyrights © The Reed Files

Published by Ophelia Bell
UNITED STATES

❦ Created with Vellum

PART I
BLACKMAIL

CHAPTER ONE

College parties bored me. I suppose they shouldn't have, but they did. Why did I still go? I wasn't exactly a social butterfly, but a girl had to keep up appearances. I was only two years into my degree and had yet to be impressed by the general atmosphere, but I wanted just enough notoriety to not be completely invisible. And I kind of liked getting laid sometimes.

College boys were easy, so I didn't exactly have to try that hard to bag one on a night like tonight. If I found the right balance of flirt versus snark, I could intrigue the smart ones. Or if one of the pretty, dumb ones caught my eye it was easy enough to play drunk and just hope he wasn't too drunk to perform once I got him into bed. The level of skill I encountered was always a crapshoot, though. Too often I would end up faking enjoyment just to get it over with quicker. At least I'd gotten pretty adept at predicting whether a guy would be worthwhile or not.

The parties were a habit for me. I went to all of them, hoping for something different each time. That's the definition of insanity, right? I must be insane.

Tonight was no different from all the others. I leaned against a wall inside a house with some combination of Greek letters emblazoned above the entrance. Fraternities amused me. They presented themselves like God's gift to women, the most virile specimens of the race, perhaps. Yet the Greeks commonly screwed adolescent boys.

They were all adolescent boys as far as I could tell. One guy in a rugby shirt was busy chugging a beer while a girl clung to him and he groped her ass. He let out a belch and a loud whoop when he was done. She cheered him on.

Ugh.

I finished my own cheap beer and went looking for something a little stronger. I had a flask in my pocket that was woefully low of tequila. My plan was to refill it where I could still get it free, then go find something more interesting. One of the bars a few blocks away had fantastic music on the weekends that none of these imbeciles would deign to pay attention to. That was more my style.

I navigated the throng of partiers to find the liquor stash. Sweet Jesus they had Patron. I silently rejoiced and filled my hungry flask.

Before the last splash hit the lip of steel and I capped it again, I heard a deep male voice that sounded way too familiar.

"Jesus, you're so hard. Take me upstairs and fuck me. Please!"

I stilled, setting the bottle back down as carefully as possible and sliding the flask back into my pocket.

Was that my stepbrother, Ben? It had sure sounded like it. But the words he'd said were entirely incongruous to the boy I'd grown up with. He was kind of a shithead, really, at least to me, but he could do no wrong in our parents' eyes. Well... his mom and my dad, who had married a decade or so ago. Ben and I never quite hit it off. I was too standoffish, and he was too irritatingly pretty. He was the popular hot jock in high school. I hated that we shared so many classes together, but I guess he was smart enough for AP classes, too. Like he needed to be smart with all those fantastically good looks. The jerk had it all, unlike me.

But what I'd just heard was something else. That was definitely his voice asking someone...some *hard* someone...to fuck him. Dare I sneak over and see who?

Of course I dared.

I took a swig straight from the Patron bottle first, of course, then corked it and set it back down. Fortification.

Then I made to leave the room with heavy steps, but paused just outside the door and stepped quietly back to the window just outside the little alcove where I'd heard the voices. I pressed my back against the molding and the curtain, flask in hand, to listen more.

Another gruff voice said, "Jesus, Ben you're on fire. I don't want to fuck you in the middle of a party."

"Andre, are you gonna make me beg?"

A deep chuckle resonated out of the alcove. Wow, Andre sounded hot. I kind of wanted to beg, too.

"No, baby. I want to, like you wouldn't believe. I just want the moment to be right." I bit my lip at the sound of that voice saying those things. This guy was a total sweetheart. So what the hell did he see in my stepbrother?

I heard more kissing and then a tiny grunt.

"Do you like that?" Ben said.

"Yeah, you've never done that before."

"I can do it again."

"Not here, alright? Let me take you home and I'll screw your brains out, or let you do whatever you want to me, too. Just not here."

"Okay, fine. But when we get back to your place, no holds barred, all right?"

No, no, no… When they got back to his place I'd miss all the fun. I'd already given up on getting laid, so I was looking for a different diversion now. Catching Ben like this had given me a genius of an idea. And torturing my stepbrother was right up my alley.

CHAPTER TWO

When I heard them moving, I moved quicker.

"Holy shit, Kat! Why are you even here?"

"Oh, just came for a little entertainment I guess. I got a nice earful of you two. Does Linette know you're gay?"

Ben's face paled. "You wouldn't…"

"I might." I loved seeing Ben's disgustingly handsome features blanch like that. It was incredibly cute, bordering on adorable enough to make me rethink my stance, but no…I had other plans.

"Do you want me to get rid of her?" Andre asked and I finally set my eyes on him. Holy shit was he a wall of muscle, and most of it very, very dark. That's where that deep voice had come from. Of course my puny little white-girl brain had to wonder what he was packing as a promise to fuck Ben with when they got out of here.

"What're you gonna do, sweetie? Fuck me silly? I might like it." I grinned at him.

"What do you want, Kat. Mom can't know about this, alright? I love him."

That declaration surprised me. Benjamin was capable of love? My heart clenched just a little bit. I might've liked my stepbrother in that moment, if I actually believed him.

"Did you always like boys?" I asked, merely out of curiosity.

"No, but Andre's not like the rest."

I glanced at Andre's looming dark body. The man was all muscle and had the coolest blue eyes. I wondered how a black guy could have blue eyes, but stranger things had happened. Andre smiled sweetly at me, with only a hint of animosity. I wondered what he'd actually do if I overtly threatened them.

Andre wasn't like the rest, Ben had said. I let that sink in. No, he wasn't like anyone I'd ever met. Ben was cute enough, and built well enough to be a ranked wrestler on our high school's team before we graduated a couple years ago.

But next to Andre he looked small. It amused me in a weird way. But the giant bulge in Andre's pants was what interested me the most.

"I'll tell you what, Ben. If you do what I ask tonight, I won't tell Linette what I saw. How's that sound?"

He seemed relieved, but a little apprehensive. He knew I was devious.

"All right… What *do* you want?"

"To watch the two of you fuck."

Andre let out a low, laugh. "She's a lot dirtier than you said she was, Ben. I think I like her."

"You talked about me?" I shot at Ben. "What the hell, dude?"

Ben gaped at me, but Andre answered, "Yeah, he alternates between calling you a slut and a prude, sweetness. I guess you two didn't know each other that well, did you?"

I kept my eyes steadily on Ben. "I guess we didn't, did we? So what is it, *brother*. Is your mom up for a rude awakening tomorrow? I'll make sure to make it as humiliating as possible."

"Jesus, Kat. I'll do anything. Do you want money?"

"You don't get it, Ben. It's your sweet humiliation I get off on the most. To see you get it up the ass by a huge black cock would be the highlight of my fucking *life*."

Andre slunk up behind him, set his hands on Ben's hips and pressed his lips against Ben's ear. "It could be fun."

"Jesus, are you on *her* side?" Ben said. "Why should I let her have the satisfaction?"

"You wanted it before she suggested we do it for an audience. So what if there's someone watching?"

Holy shit, that voice. No wonder Ben wanted the man's cock. Mesmerizing didn't even begin to cover it.

"Because she's my *sister*," Ben said, but this time he lacked the conviction he'd had earlier.

Andre darted a look at me and smiled. I smiled back. He was on board. And then he did something entirely unexpected—he reached into Ben's pants, grabbed his cock and apparently gave it a nice hard squeeze.

"Alright, alright!" Ben yelped. His sculpted cheekbones flushed beneath his wide blue eyes. "Can we go to your place? My roommate isn't really cool…"

"Yeah, baby. My place is good."

"You're going to pay for this, Kat. Somehow," Ben shot at me as the three of us moved toward the door.

"Ooh, that's a nice threat, brother. I can't wait." I smacked him hard on the ass and followed the pair to an SUV parked at the curb.

CHAPTER THREE

Some of the best plans happen on the fly. This was probably one of my more genius ideas. At least it seemed that way. I was generally horny but the average college man just wasn't going to cut it to satisfy me. This entire plan was just a diversion I could masturbate to later. The fact that it would humiliate and traumatize my golden stepbrother in the process was just icing on the cake.

He was a prop as far as I was concerned. I hoped that the looks Andre had given me were indication enough of what he'd like to do later. The man had definitely given me some looks that made my panties wet. So I'd watch Ben take it in the ass, then when he passed out from exhaustion, maybe Andre and I could have a private moment. Yet another bit of ammo I could hold over Ben's head afterward.

Andre drove us to a swanky apartment in a nicer

part of town. I almost wondered if he was a drug dealer until I saw the football trophies and memorabilia everywhere and it finally clicked who he was. My stupid stepbrother had actually managed to fall in bed with a pro? That boggled my mind. I'd probably be even more impressed if I followed sports. Either way, the guy was clearly slumming it, going to a frat party with Ben.

"Kitty Kat, want a drink?"

I turned to the sound of Andre's deep voice. He held a carton of half and half in his hand and shook it with a wicked grin.

"Fuck you," I said.

He poured anyway, mixing the milk with Kahlua and vodka. I wasn't particularly a fan of sweet drinks, but I appreciated the gesture.

Ben tossed his own back fast and had another two in quick succession.

"Would it be easier if I just called mommy now?" I asked in my sweetest, most condescending tone.

"No. You wanted this, you got it. Come on, Andre, it's time."

Andre laughed. "If you're ready, I am."

I followed them into Andre's bedroom. Andre glanced at me a few times while he lit candles, his gaze curious. I kept giving him the same sly smile even though I was suddenly nervous.

The reality of it all was starting to sink in. I was about to blackmail my own stepbrother into letting this guy nail him in front of me. I knew he wanted it, and I really, really wanted to see it. Yet it sat wrong somehow. Sure, my stepbrother was a jerk and probably deserved it on some level, but this was the same guy I'd grown up with—the same guy I'd reluctantly spent the last ten Christmases with, both of us trying to one-up the other on the worst gift ever.

Ben glared at me the entire time. Finally Andre whispered something to him and he calmed. The looming shape of Andre approached with a chair. "Sit here, Kat," he said. "And if you're gonna watch us get naked, I think it's only fair if you're naked, too. What d'you say?"

He lifted the hem of his t-shirt right in front of me and smiled as he pulled it over his head and peeled the fabric down his thick arms. I eyed his pecs and licked my lips. He had the letters of one of the Black fraternities on campus literally *branded* into his left pec. I knew tattoos hurt. I had a few of my own in strategic spots my dad would never see, but I couldn't imagine actually being branded like that. The idea that he was tough enough to withstand it made me all the more eager to watch him nail Ben.

Then he unfastened his jeans and I stood mesmerized, waiting for the reveal. He paused with his zipper half down and raised his hand, making a little "get on with it" gesture at me.

"Jesus, Andre, can we just get this over with?" Ben shot from behind Andre. He was standing by the bed with his arms crossed over his chest looking even more anxious than before.

"Hold tight, baby," he said without removing his gaze from me. "I just want to make sure the experience is worth it for her. Less likelihood of her reneging, right?" His smile widened at me. "Now, if you want to see more of us, we need to see more of you," he said in an even deeper voice that somehow managed to vibrate from my eardrums all the way to my clit.

Without a word, I nodded and unbuttoned my shirt. My face heated under Andre's gaze and I was grateful for the dim candlelight in the room to cover up my embarrassment. I wasn't exactly an exhibitionist and having two pairs of male eyes observe the proceedings was completely alien to me. Particularly when one was Ben.

When I got my shirt off and went for the button of my jeans, Andre resumed his own disrobing.

"Wait," I said, before he could continue. "It's not quite fair for him to still have his clothes on."

Andre gave me a sly smile, then moved to my stepbrother's side and began undressing him. He tugged Ben's shirt over his head, sliding his hands over Ben's tight stomach in the process. Ben was apparently no slouch when it came to working out. He looked nicer than I imagined with his clothes off. Much nicer when Andre pushed his pants down and I got an eyeful of Ben's already hard cock.

The sight made my mouth water and I swallowed. I

should *not* be attracted to the sight of my stepbrother's hard dick. I forced my eyes back to Andre, suddenly uncertain about my entire plan.

"He's got a nice one, doesn't he?" Andre said. "Tastes as good as it looks."

"Jesus, man," Ben shot at Andre. "She's my stepsister. Don't talk about my dick, all right?"

Andre chuckled. "It isn't a lie. And I think she likes it anyway. Isn't that true, Kitty Kat?"

I scrambled for a coherent response. Finally I chose to affect vague interest. I raised an eyebrow, looked pointedly at Ben's hard dick that I kind of really wanted to rub my tongue on, and said, "It'll do, I guess."

"Will it do enough to entertain you while I fuck him?"

I tore my eyes away from Ben's cock and stared at Andre. "What?"

"You want to watch me fuck him in the ass, right? But I want to watch *you* jerk him off while I do it. Or let him fuck you. Your choice."

Ben and I both made sounds of intense displeasure. "Fuck that last part. Fuck all of it," Ben said. "She wants to watch... that's all she's doing."

Andre made a soft "tsk tsk" with is tongue. "Baby, if you want to keep getting my cock I really need to see this."

The absolute depravity of the idea shocked me, but at the same time my pussy ached for it to actually happen. I was close to saying yes, but I wasn't sure Ben was yet.

"Fine. I'll..." I had a hard time saying it. Mostly because I was conflicted about the options I was given. It wasn't about Ben...but that cock. He had a really beautiful cock. I think I might've been in love. It was thick where the base nestled in the coarse gold curls, and curved in a perfect arc. I'd had no idea he wasn't circumcised, but that made it all the more beautiful. His foreskin wrapped around the head, with just enough of his tip showing that I could see the bead of moisture clinging to him. I imagined myself licking him until he begged me to let him shove his cock into me.

"I want him to fuck me." My entire torso heated with the confession, but I kept my eyes on Ben just to see how he reacted.

"What the *fuck*?"

"What? Are you afraid of me?" I asked, point blank. Ben and I locked eyes. His pretty blues looked terrified, but the rest of his body told a different story when I gave it a slow once-over. His cock was hard, a rivulet of moisture dripping from his tip and creeping down the underside. His nipples were as hard as mine were, too. I wanted to suck on all of him. Goddamn him for being my stepbrother. If he hadn't been, I'd probably already have had him.

"No..." he said. He sounded uncertain.

"He's scared he'll like it," Andre interjected.

"All the better if he does," I said. Blackmail was blackmail and suddenly the idea held even more weight than before. Ben's uncertainty spurred me on, but it worried me a little that Andre was so enthusiastic about the whole thing. Still, I got into the game of torturing Ben. It helped that Andre's voice was the thing spurring me on. Every time he spoke, the low cadence of it made my nipples tingle.

"Take off your bra, Kat," Andre said.

His voice had me too enthralled not to follow his command.

My full breasts sprang free with a twitch of my fingers at my back and I let the bra slip off my arms. When I looked up, Ben was eyeing me like he might eat me. Christ, did the sight of my body actually turn him on? Should I be disturbed by that? I didn't even care if he'd tell my dad about the tattoo of a dragon I had that swirled darkly around one breast. It was too big to deny, yet he didn't say a word or react in any way aside from a twitch of his cock.

It took a nudge from Andre for Ben to tear his eyes off me. As strange as the entire moment had felt, I was a little sad he stopped looking. It seemed like the first time he'd ever actually *seen* me since we'd met a decade ago when our parents started dating.

"You're hard for her, huh? Your stepsister's pretty tits do it for you more than I do?" Andre asked with mock offense. He looked back at me with a grin. "Why don't you finish getting undressed, then come over here and get a feel of him?" Andre said. As if in illustration, he cupped Ben's balls and then gave his cock a long, languid stroke.

I kicked off my boots and shimmied out of my jeans and panties. I'd started this demented little game, and damn if seeing Ben squirm didn't get me hot.

Ben's mouth fell open and his eyes widened in surprise as I approached. I'd seen him do the same thing when we watched movies together as kids. I always found it adorable that such a total hottie like him was affected the way he was by those moments. This was a little different, though.

"You're not actually going to…" he backed up but Andre was behind him preventing his escape.

"Oh, you bet I am," I said.

Andre removed his hand from Ben's cock and I reached out. Ben's hips twitched backward, but Andre grabbed him tightly and held him, whispering in his ear. "You want this as much as you wanted me. Just admit it."

I had the strangest urge to make gentle cooing sounds to calm him, then remembered that was the last thing I wanted. The more agitated he became, the more fun it would be for me. So I shifted even closer until my nipples brushed his chest and I could gaze up into his eyes while I continued the sweet torture. My nipples tingled deliciously at the contact and my hands itched to touch him even more. The loud thrum of my pulse in my ears made it harder to focus now, but this was absolutely already happening. I was about to touch my stepbrother's cock and I loved it.

"Oh, God, Kat," he practically moaned the words when I cupped his balls with my hand. I followed the same slow stroke that Andre had done, except I drew it out, squeezed a little tighter, and then let my thumb swirl around his tip, spreading the moisture.

He made a little strangled noise in his throat and gazed down at me like I might be the most incredible thing he'd ever seen. He looked at me like he'd looked at the image of a constellation magnified through the observatory telescope to see the utmost detail. The love of astronomy was one of the few things we had in common. I almost wanted to tell him I wasn't Andromeda, so he could close his mouth. The sight of his tongue slipping over his lips when his gaze drifted to my pussy made me shiver.

Cool air from a draft tickled across the bare skin that I'd religiously waxed ever since it started growing. I hated having hair there. But the thing I knew Ben fixated on was the tattoo that I had in place of a bush.

That had been a fun day, followed by an incredibly satisfying fuck with the tattoo artist. He'd nailed me from behind, 'to avoid irritating the area'. I didn't give a shit. He was a hot guy, but anonymous sex is anonymous sex. Not having to look in his eyes when he came was preferable considering I barely knew his name.

Watching Ben's reaction while he stared at my pussy was mesmerizing.

"Do you want to lick her?" Andre asked.

Ben seemed to think a moment. Thankfully... I didn't know the answer either. Not anymore.

Then he licked his lips and nodded his head very slowly. "Like you wouldn't fucking believe," he said.

"What?" I blurted it out without thinking. "You want to ...?"

Ben's face twisted in an irritated grimace. "Jesus, Kat. Will you let me love you for once?"

His words left me numb. I couldn't *not* think about what they meant. I just stood there, stunned, while my stepbrother knelt between my thighs. He didn't just drop to his knees, though. He raised his hands and cupped my breasts first, then kind of *melted* down my body with his mouth kissing and licking the entire way and his hands sliding down my sides until they reached around and squeezed my ass.

Each bit of warm contact made it painfully clear to me that somehow my plan was going to hell. I had no idea how to rein it back in, or even if I wanted to.

CHAPTER FOUR

When Ben was finally face-to-pussy he looked at it like he'd just had a nice date with my snatch and wanted to give it a memorable kiss good night. And then his lips were suddenly pressed against me, his tongue buried as deep as it would go. The invasion happened so fast I could barely process the intense, unexpected sensation of his eager tongue slipping between my folds.

"I kind of thought you were gay," I whispered to the top of his head when I could finally catch my breath. I threaded my fingers through his hair and clenched it tight after the first sweet flick against my clit. He was good…too good. He seemed to know precisely what pattern to lick that would blow my mind. I didn't want him to stop, but I hated that I loved it so much.

"Oh, fuck, Ben. This is so wrong," I said when it started to feel way too nice to deny. Like it would've been okay to have my stepbrother lick my pussy if I didn't enjoy it.

Ben chuckled against me. "Yeah, it is. That's why I love it. That's why I love you."

I froze at the words. "Ben? You don't really mean that, do you?"

He paused and spoke into my snatch, his lips brushing me with each word. "I've loved you for a decade, Kat. You've just been such a bitch I didn't have the balls to tell you. Andre knew." He glanced over his shoulder at the man who had apparently betrayed me.

"I'm not going to *fuck* you…you're my stepbrother!" I pulled away from him, suddenly too conscious that I'd lost control of the situation. It was one thing to suggest doing it to toy with him, but now that the tables had turned I was scrambling to figure out how to get out of it.

"You just had my tongue in your snatch, Kat!" Ben yelled from his solitary kneeling position on the floor where I'd left him.

"Yeah, and it was nice, but you're still a fucking asshole!"

As adamant as I was about it, my libido had other ideas. I hadn't quite come from his glorious tongue, though he'd gotten me close. And I kind of hated Andre for orchestrating the entire thing and then standing back to watch the fallout. He was still there, with that stupid, sexy grin of his, and I was furious about all of it.

"You! You bastard!" I launched myself at Andre. "Did you plan this? Did you know already?"

Andre laughed and grabbed my wrists. He was too strong for me and I fell against him. It took a second for me to remember that I was actually still naked, and he was very much aware of it. He held me against him, his soft lips whispering, "Let him make love to you. He needs it."

"He's my brother," I murmured.

"Not really...I know that much," he whispered. "He needs to get over you to be with me, though. I love him and you're just standing in the way, sweetness. So just let him, alright?"

He kept a tight hold on me and pulled me toward the bed. He lowered himself onto it and lay back, holding me tight to his chest while he did. The motion left me prone on top of him, chest-to-chest, and I could feel the hard press of his cock through his jeans against my hip

It was the first time I'd been that close to him and I was suddenly overwhelmed by the intimacy of the situation.

"Why don't you fuck us both?" I turned my head and gave Ben a questioning glance over my shoulder. "You want it, don't you, Kat? I want to see you come undone while I fuck you. If that means sharing you with Andre..." He smiled. "Well, I'll gladly share."

It occurred to me suddenly that I could get out of this the same way I got into it...I could threaten to tell my stepmother her son was gay just to keep him from fucking me.

"You don't have to do this, Ben. Mom doesn't need to know you're a deviant perv if you just stop now..."

"Is that why you're so wet?" he asked. His fingers slipped deep into me from behind. "Jesus, Kat. Did I do that to you? Who's the deviant perv?" He chuckled and pressed his fingers deeper.

"Fuck you, Ben." I only managed to get the words out before I lost my breath completely. His fingers made me want to whimper and squirm at how good they felt but Andre still held me too tight to gain any traction. Andre chuckled and tilted his hips up into me.

My mind was turning to mush under Ben's touch. He stroked his thumb against my asshole and did something incredibly delicious with his fingers just as he slipped his thumb past my puckered opening. I couldn't repress the cry of pleasure, but I also couldn't let this go on. I spread my legs wider—to give myself more leverage to get away, is what I told myself—but it left me even more exposed. At that same second one of Andre's hands moved between us to finish unzipping his jeans and pull out his cock. The hot length of it pressed into my belly and I tilted my hips reflexively, aching to feel his hot, smooth skin rub me in the same spot that Ben was already teasing relentlessly

"You like that, huh?" Ben asked. "How would you like both of us inside this tight pussy of yours?"

My clit throbbed and I twitched my hips again, trying my best to angle enough to brush the sensitive bundle against Andre's cock. I needed to rub on something, that's for sure. I squirmed until one of my arms made it between us and I could finally reach down and wrap my fingers around that glorious, thick shaft.

Andre moaned at the stroke I gave him and sank his teeth into my shoulder. He was becoming less of a target and more of a hindrance to me getting at Ben, though. I was too aware of the presence of those fingers, especially now that Ben had what felt like all four of them buried deep in my pussy while his thumb still worked at my asshole. And I couldn't shake the idea of his beautiful cock still looming back there, hard as a rock and ready to sink into me.

I hadn't done this to get my rocks off as much as I had to humiliate my stupid stepbrother, but here I was, held down with him fingering me to distraction.

"Are you gonna come like this, Kat? Or would you rather come on my cock? Why don't we try that now?"

"Oh, God, Ben. We can't." Even as I said it, my body betrayed me. My hand stroked Andre faster and my pussy clenched hard around Ben's fingers. He was perilously close to actually making me come and the mere suggestion of having him fuck me to climax made me even wetter. As lovely a cock as my stepbrother had, my craving him was just as much about how very wrong it was to want him inside me.

"I think we can. Turn her over, Andre."

CHAPTER FIVE

The huge, dark arms that held me shifted and gripped my shoulders. Andre turned me like a rag doll and I didn't even resist. My ass came to rest against his pelvis and his cock sprang loose between my legs, canting slightly to the right and resting hotly against my thigh. He scooted us both farther back on the bed, every flex of his muscular chest tickling against my back.

I got a nice view of Ben from that angle. He seemed like a stranger to me now, though. I didn't see my jerk-face of a stepbrother anymore. I saw the lean muscled strength of an athlete and a lovely face flushed with lust. His blue eyes blazed with desire and my entire body tingled under his gaze. He was targeting *me* with that look, and gently stroking his own cock while he did it.

"Do you have any idea how many times I've jerked

off thinking about having you just like this?" he asked. "God, you are so beautiful and you don't even seem to know. I think that's the thing I love most. That and your epic tits. I don't think I've ever met a woman who has tits as spectacular as yours are. And fuck if that tattoo doesn't make them even more gorgeous."

I couldn't even respond. I was too anxious about the way he casually sauntered closer while he spoke, until the bed dipped from him climbing on and straddling my legs where they were pinned by Andre's. But when he made the comment about my tits, I heard Andre murmur a sound of agreement in my ear and his embrace of me shifted. Both his hands slid higher and cupped my breasts, thumbs sweeping over my already hard and sensitive nipples.

"That's right," Ben said, his lips curling into a wicked, hungry smile. He leaned over me, bracing his arms on either side. I don't know what it was that made me moan from pleasure the most—the fact that his cock slid along the top of my pussy or his lips wrapping around one of my nipples. He rolled the hard nub around with his tongue and Andre whispered in my ear. "You like that tongue of his, don't you?"

Yeah, I did. But it was something else that made my mind go blank from pleasure. With one hand Ben gripped his cock and swiped the tip up and down between my lust-wettened folds, then pressed it teasingly at my entrance.

"This is it, Kat," he said, pulling back and looking directly in my eyes. "Tell me you want me. Tell me you want my cock."

I did squirm and whimper then, just to get closer. I was having a really hard time figuring out how to actually articulate words as simple as, "Yes, please fuck me, Ben." My pussy ached to have him in me. As if sensing my need, Andre hooked both his feet around my lower legs and spread me wider.

"She's ready, aren't you, Kitty Kat? I can feel your pussy juice leaking all over me."

"Yes," I finally managed to squeak out just as Ben tilted his hips and thrust into me a tiny bit. It couldn't have been more than the first inch or two of his cock, but the sweet stretch of him finally being in me made me cry out.

"Oh, fuck, you're tight. And here I thought you were such a little slut the last few years. I hated the idea of anyone else ever fucking you. How many men have you fucked, Kat?"

Jesus, he wanted to have a conversation? I twitched my hips trying to get him in deeper, but he smirked and pulled back.

"You want more of me, you've gotta spill. How many?"

I wracked my brain. There had been a handful but none so well endowed as my stepbrother or Andre. And it had probably been a year since the last guy—the tattooist. Hence my urge to go on the hunt tonight. It'd been too long a dry spell.

"A few? I don't know. And for the record I fucking hate you. Now will you just fuck me?"

"Only if you promise me something. Promise me after tonight only my cock gets to be inside you. Because I'll fucking kill any other man who touches you."

I heard a throat clearing right in my ear. Ben glanced at Andre and smiled. "Well, me or Andre, I guess."

I doubted I could hold to a promise like that but I wanted him so badly I nodded. The sweet, slow friction of his cock sinking into me made me flutter my eyelids in pleasure.

"Ben...Oh, God..." Before I could get out more words his mouth descended on mine, his tongue invading with its sweet, coffee flavor from the drinks he'd downed earlier. The flavor hit me in the most abstract way as I kissed him back. Somehow I expected my stepbrother the pretty frat boy to taste like beer.

More than that, though, the feel of his mouth claiming mine shattered my former impressions of him as the irritating, too-pretty, too-arrogant stepbrother I'd grown up with. The kiss was desperate, hungry, and full of promise. Then his cock plunged into me with a sudden, swift thrust and all the broken pieces of that old impression were swept away like detritus in a strong wind.

I clung to him with both hands, devouring his kiss with my own hungry lips. Andre's hands shifted, one still clutching my breast and teasing my nipple, while the other moved somewhere beyond my field of vision. It wasn't until I felt his cock shift along my inner thigh that I realized what he was after.

Ben realized it at the same time, and slowed his fucking, pulling out long enough to help. I watched down my pinned torso as Ben gripped Andre's huge black cock and stroked it once. He aimed the tip at my pussy and swirled the swollen head around my slick clit, the sensation sending swift jolts of pleasure through my body.

Holy shit, he knew what he was doing, and he wasn't ready to stop there.

He slid his own shaft against Andre's and held them tight in one fist, one dark and one light, aiming them both at my hungry pussy. The slow stretch of both cocks entering me hurt at first, but I was so wet, they only had to thrust a little to sink deeper. Once both tips slipped inside me, I think my brain shut down from the pleasure of them filling me to my utmost limits.

I was nothing but a moaning ball of intense pleasure when Ben eased himself down onto me and shoved harder into my aching snatch. At the same time,

Andre thrust from beneath, the pair of them finding an agonizing rhythm that threatened to destroy my sanity the way every millimeter of my sensitive channel was being rubbed while they fucked me.

Andre's hand slipped around and found my clit. He murmured harsh filth in my ear as his cock shoved deeper and his fingers rubbed the needy little nub in just the right way.

"You like these two big cocks filling you up, don't you? Jesus, Kitty Kat, your pussy is so sweet and tight, I can't wait to get a taste of it when we're done. I'm gonna lick our cum right out of you."

The words cascaded through me in a low rumble, the sounds vibrating through his chest and into my ears. The very idea of what he suggested was too much on top of all the other sensations my body was bombarded with. The fullness of both huge cocks invading me relentlessly had me ready to surrender. My pussy tingled and pulsed under Andre's steady attention and my muscles clenched around both cocks as I let go with a quavering moan.

"That's right, Kat. Give it up. Oh, Christ I'm ready to shoot my load in you." Ben's gaze held mine, his brow glistening with sweat.

I lost control of my body when it happened. Both of them let out loud grunts and groans at the same time when my muscles spasmed, my entire lower body seizing up. My orgasm seemed like a living thing invading my body. It took hold in an instant and held me in a tight embrace. Then left behind a remnant of need. Not need for pleasure, though…what it left behind was a need for love.

Ben raised a hand and clutched at my hair, lowering his mouth to mine again and plunging his tongue between my lips in a desperate kiss while his cock pulsed inside me.

The entire world disappeared in that moment. I may have actually passed out from the pleasure, but one stark thought kept going through my head: "I think I'm in love with my stepbrother."

CHAPTER SIX

When I finally opened my eyes, Ben was still hovering over me, his own eyes wide with amazement. His arms began to shake from the effort and he finally moved, rolling off me and laying on the bed staring up at the ceiling. Andre shifted beneath me.

"Slowly, Kitty Kat. I'd like to feel you for a second all to myself," he said. He pushed back into me with a couple lazy thrusts, before extracting his flagging cock and releasing me. A very vivid emptiness was left behind now that both of them had vacated my body.

Andre gently rolled me off him and disappeared through a doorway on the other side of the room. I lay on my side, staring at my stepbrother.

"Did you mean everything you said?" I asked softly. I wasn't a very trusting person, as a general rule. In fact, it was Ben's fault that I wasn't, after all the cruel pranks he used to pull on me when we were younger. I generally gave as good as I got, but his confessions tonight had added an unexpected layer of perspective to our entire childhood.

"I think it's the first time I haven't lied to you," he said. He turned his head to look at me. For the first time in my life, he looked terrified.

"Jesus, Ben. Have you been holding this inside you all these years?"

"Do you hate me now? More than you did before, I mean."

I reached out a tentative hand and placed it on his chest, trying to ignore the way I shook as I did. He reached up and gripped my hand tightly.

"I guess I wish I'd known," I said.

He let out a shaky laugh. "It's not like we could've done much before. I just knew when the idea of a perfect woman came up that you were it for me. It kind of broke my heart that you couldn't stand to be around me."

"What about Andre?"

"He's the perfect man for me."

I raised an eyebrow. His bold declaration made my esteem of him rise a few notches.

"He is…amazing," I said, remembering every little subtle piece of Andre's part in the game thus far. He was good at being the director in the background, handing cues to the both of us. I kind of wanted to reward him for it. Give him the focus he deserved.

"I love you both," Ben said softly. "Is that fucked up? I mean, what would Mom say if she knew what a fucking pervert I am? I'm in love with two people…a gorgeous black man for one…and my own stepsister."

He looked so tortured by the revelation my heart ached.

"Ben, sweetie…" I climbed on top of him and stared down into those big blue eyes I'd always hated seeing but kind of loved like crazy just now. "For one thing, Andre is a work of art. Loving him is a no-brainer. Why you'd love me is confusing and makes no fucking sense. We've always hated each other."

"Maybe you hated me. I always loved you. I just hated that you didn't love me back."

I kissed him instead of crying on him. My beautiful stepbrother was apparently capable of saying very sweet things that totally disarmed me. His arms wrapped around me and the world tilted. When he had me on my back he raised up and looked into my eyes.

"I've always loved you and I always will. Please stay with us?"

"Us?" I asked.

The thundering rumble of a voice came from across the room. "He means me."

I turned my head to look. Andre stood entirely naked, leaning against the doorframe of the bathroom. The dim candlelight gleamed on his smooth, dark muscles. He shifted to grip the doorframe behind him, leaving his entire torso uncovered. The light played down his body all the way to his flaccid cock that hung like a heavy weight between his legs. The man was truly beautiful. And now he seemed like he was hanging on my answer as much as Ben was.

I had no idea how to respond. The pair had just banged me silly and now they were both asking for more. None of the other men I'd had sex with had showed any more interest in me than "let's do this again sometime."

"What do you want? Just to fuck sometimes?"

I directed the question at Andre, but Ben answered. "No. We want you. Kind of forever."

"Kind of forever...Jesus, Ben, that sounds..." How did it sound? Incredibly romantic and sweet. My brain imploded a little at that idea. Romantic and sweet weren't part of my own dialog. I hated that shit. Yet I wanted to cry and hug Ben for suggesting it at all. The fact that he thought about me that way melted my heart. I was surprised I hadn't turned into a puddle of goo already.

"How does it sound, Kat?"

I glanced between him and Andre, thinking. But who was I kidding, really?

"It sounds kind of perfect."

PART II
BETRAYAL

CHAPTER SEVEN

I used to think I knew what great sex felt like. I'd had plenty of it in my twenty-two years, with a variety of partners. Mostly men, but when you're a horny college girl, sometimes experimentation can be its own reward. It had all been pretty fantastic, as far as I knew. I enjoyed it enough, but nothing had ever really blown my mind.

That is, until I hooked up with my stepbrother, Ben, and his hot athlete of a lover, Andre. The first night we were together surprised me. Not only because that was the night my irritating asshole stepbrother confessed his undying love for me. It was also the night I learned how fantastic sex could be when you were falling head over heels for someone.

Ben and I had never been particularly close, unless you counted our mutual goal of tormenting each other with crude insults and mean jokes throughout our lives. I was too much of an angry outcast and he was too much of a pretty boy jock. We'd been at each other's throats since our parents married when we were both twelve years old. I suppose love and hate are just two sides of the same coin, though, and that first night was when Ben made a different call on the flip. And somehow we both came up winners.

Andre was a happy bonus, really, but he had also been the choreographer that night. I don't think the night would have gone as spectacularly as it had if he hadn't been involved, urging Ben to come clean and tell me how he really felt.

In the end we all ended up together, happily shacking up in Andre's swanky apartment in one of the richer parts of town, not far from where our parents lived.

Of course our parents were none the wiser. My stepmother's reaction would have been bad enough if she knew that I was regularly getting fucked by a large black man. She likely would have had an aneurysm had she discovered I was also screwing her beautiful, perfect son on a nightly basis.

And I absolutely loved every mindblowingly orgasmic moment of it.

CHAPTER EIGHT

"Come for me baby, that's right," Andre's deep murmur sank into my ear over the sound of the shower streaming down around us. His voice seemed to burrow straight to my clit. My hips twitched, pressing my needy snatch tighter against Ben's mouth as he knelt between my legs. Andre tweaked one nipple, then swirled soapy fingertips around it before cupping my breast and squeezing. It was incredibly difficult not to fly apart, with two fingers of Andre's other hand sunk deep in my ass while Ben's tongue lapped at my pussy with quick, perfectly targeted sweeps. Close ... so close. They'd gotten theirs before we got into the shower, and now it was my turn finally. And boy was this orgasm going to be good.

I tilted my head back against Andre's shoulder and

let my hand rest on Ben's wet head. One of his hands gripped my hips while the other held my right thigh steady where it draped over his shoulder. I grew weak from the pleasure and relinquished my body to their touch, relishing the slow build of pleasure that accumulated between my thighs.

The door buzzer sounded loudly from the front of the apartment. Ben jerked his head back in surprise, his eyes wide with alarm.

"Fuck!" he yelled, coming to his senses while I stood there, too addled from ecstasy to even register why he was so upset. He launched himself out of the shower and sprinted out the door, pausing only to grab a towel on the way.

"Ben! You fucker, get back here! I'm not finished!"

"No worries, baby, I've got you covered," Andre said. He rinsed the hand off that had been teasing at my breasts and slid his arm down my torso like a python, sinking his fingers into me from the front while the fingers of his other hand still worked in and out of my ass.

Then it hit me like splash of icy water. There was only one reason Ben would have moved that fast to get the door.

"Fuck!" I yelled, echoing Ben's earlier outburst. I groaned and pushed Andre's hands away, hurriedly rinsed, and darted out of the shower.

"Suit yourself," Andre said. He turned the hot water

up and stood beneath the steaming showerhead while I grabbed a towel and ran after Ben, leaving another pair of wet footprints across the wood floor of the master bedroom the three of us shared.

Ben was already dressed and gone, and I heard two voices from the front room. Ben's was clear, his tone slightly high pitched the way it would get when he was stressed out. The other voice was the familiar haughty, affected lilt of my stepmother, Linette. I peeked out the bedroom door, but neither of them were in sight, so I took a chance and sprinted across the hallway to the guest room where I kept the majority of my things. There were three bedrooms and bathrooms in the apartment, but only the master was ever used. With its king-sized bed, cushy furniture, and ample floor space, it was ideal for the kinds of fun the three of us preferred to have on a regular basis.

Linette didn't need to be clued in to our arrangement, however. I had a vivid image in my mind of the horrified, disgusted look she would give me if she saw me exiting the bedroom she already knew belonged to the swarthy, athletic owner of the apartment Ben and I supposedly sublet.

What she didn't know was that Andre refused to accept rent from us. His dad had been some rich, hotshot pro football player who died of cancer a few years earlier and left Andre his entire fortune. Andre had told us once that before his dad died, he'd said his only wish for Andre was that he find love and hold onto it like his life depended on it. I think that was one of his ways to try to hold onto us, but he didn't really need to try that hard. We weren't going anywhere, even if he charged us rent to live with him.

So instead of paying rent, Ben and I had secretly pooled our college housing allowance into a joint savings account, "for a rainy day" as Ben said. I loved him for his little schemes now as much as I used to hate him for them when we were growing up.

I was still half dressed and in the middle of plaiting my long, wet hair into a neat, thick braid when Ben popped his own head through my door without knocking.

"Get a move on, Kat. She's got reservations at that pretentious cafe she loves so much."

I shot an irritated look at him. "You're an asshole, Ben. I didn't even *know* she was coming. When did you plan on telling me?"

"I did tell you. Three days ago when we were out."

"You mean when I was three sheets to the wind and the two of you were busy going down on me in the ladies room at the club?"

"Just before that," he said.

I snorted and threw my hairbrush at him, then began to shoot a successive volley of elastic hair ties toward his head. He laughed and shut the door to ward off my attack.

I hurriedly threw on some makeup and took a

second to survey myself in the mirror. Linette would at least be pleased that I chose to wear a pretty, girly sundress and had my hair up. Hopefully that would appease her after having to wait.

After slipping on a pair of strappy, stacked-heel shoes I knew she'd also approve of more than my usual dark leather boots, I sauntered into the living room and smiled sunnily at the older woman who sat in a fake relaxed posture on our dark leather sofa.

"Mom! Ben forgot to tell me we had a date. What a great surprise!"

She probably knew I was full of shit, especially because I never called her "Mom" unless I was lying to her, but she liked it when I made an effort to keep up appearances.

Even though she'd attempted to raise me and be a good maternal figure for the last ten years, she and I had never managed to find any common ground outside of loving my dad. I mentally edited that thought to include Ben, too. At least within the last few months my feelings toward Ben had done a one-eighty, which I think pleased her to no end. It also pleased me that she had no clue about the true nature of my "love" for Ben, or his for me.

She returned my fake smile with one of her own and stood to hug me.

As I was about to step toward her and accept her embrace, a sharp smack hit my backside and I jumped.

Andre's deep voice whispered in my ear, "I'll make

sure you don't go hungry tonight, Kitty Kat, if you promise not to run away." In a louder voice, he said, "Nice to see you again, Mrs. Farrell. I wish I could join you for breakfast, but practice calls."

My face heated in response and my ass tingled pleasantly under his palm, which he had the audacity to leave there for the next few seconds while he offered his other hand in greeting to Linette. I hoped like hell Linette couldn't see Andre groping me, but I had no doubt she'd heard the smack from the way her eyes narrowed and her lips pressed briefly into a tight line.

She recovered quickly and accepted his offered hand, but the set of her mouth made her distaste very apparent. I think if Andre hadn't been loaded and the owner of the apartment we shared, she'd have probably railed against us even being friends with the guy, much less living with him. My stuck up WASP of a stepmother wasn't the most enlightened individual.

With a final little squeeze Andre released my ass cheek. I let out the breath I'd been holding and forced myself not to watch him walk toward the front door with his duffel of gear slung over one huge shoulder. When I glanced back at Linette, her gaze seemed fixed on something in that direction, too. I smiled to myself while I watched her watch Andre's ass flex under his track pants. Yeah, those solid mounds of muscle were like twin magnets for a woman's eyes. And many men's eyes, too, for that matter.

"Mom, are you ready?" Ben asked, a hint of humor in his voice. He and I shared an amused look at her flustered reaction. She regained her composure quickly and nodded. "We may just make it in time for our reservation."

CHAPTER NINE

Having to endure Linette's critical eye had always made me feel tiny and insignificant growing up. Yet somehow today none of it seemed to faze me. Perhaps it was the secret Ben and I shared that had finally given me power over the woman. Where I used to believe the two of them both hated me and had it out for me my whole life, now I knew that Ben was actually on my side and had been all along.

Every so often on the way to the restaurant, he would accidentally brush up against me—a fingertip brushing an imagined speck of lint off the shoulder of my thin sweater, or a hand pressed at my lower back as he accompanied me through a door. Each time he touched me, my entire body felt like it was vibrating.

Christ, I was tense. I had desperately needed that orgasm, but now I was trapped, forced to endure a meal with my least favorite person in the world. As if he sensed my tension, Ben briefly grabbed my hand out of view of his mother and squeezed. I let out a small sigh and shot him a smile of gratitude. Yes, he was definitely on my side, and I loved him desperately for that. Almost as much as I wanted to skip this tedious brunch ahead of us and drag him back to bed for the day.

When Linette was dealing with the valet at the restaurant, Ben bent his head to whisper in my ear, "I wish I was having you for breakfast."

I shot him an irritated look. "You *did*, you just didn't clean your plate, you ass."

He leaned away from me and grinned. "Ooh, someone sounds a little frustrated. Is there anything I can do to help with that, Kat?"

"You can shut up, is what you can do. She's coming." Sometimes I wondered if Ben got off on the prospect of getting caught in the act. I'd caught him with Andre that night months ago, and thought I'd finally had something to hold over his head that he couldn't worm his way out of. That plan had backfired spectacularly, though. Not that I was complaining now.

Yet as sweet and attentive as he'd become since that night, he still had a mischievous streak when it came to me. Some things never changed.

As much as I loved Ben's attention, it didn't quite distract me from the rising dread of the true purpose of this outing with Linette. She had the familiar smug look she only got when she was about to fuck with my life. She'd done it several times over the years and I still hadn't managed to figure out how to avoid her schemes.

After the hostess seated us and our waiter had taken our drink orders, Linette wasted no time on her personal agenda. If there was one thing I'd learned about the woman over the years, she had a reason for every single conversation she had with either me or Ben. I'd known this visit couldn't possibly be simply to spend time with us. I wasn't quite prepared for what she offered next. After a preamble so full of bullshit I was afraid she'd offend the other diners, she finally got to the point.

"Katherine, you need to consider your future after college. Benjamin is already on a solid path toward his law degree. But you still seem ... aimless. So your father and I have arranged an internship for you with a friend of a colleague of mine. It begins Monday and lasts for the rest of the summer and through the next year until you graduate. We thought it was time for you to gain some hands on experience in your field."

As she spoke, my fingers began curling into claws against my thighs, nails digging into my skin. I clenched my jaw. Could I get away with clawing the woman's eyes out in this fancy restaurant? Ben must have sensed my mood shift, because a second later I felt his hand reach under the tablecloth and squeeze my knee gently. Unfortunately this was one situation where his touch didn't break through my irritation.

"What the fuck did you do Linette?"

She didn't even bat an eye, the bitch. "Trust me, my dear, this is good for you. So you'll need to pack tomorrow. Your ticket's already paid for and an apartment is rented."

Before I could say anything, Ben piped up. "Mom! You didn't even *ask* what she wanted! It's not fair for you to spring bullshit like this on her. And why the hell isn't Dad here to tell her himself? Where are you trying to send her anyway?"

"Benjamin, I appreciate the fact that you two have overcome your differences finally after all these years of fighting, but you have to understand we are looking out for your sister's welfare. This will be a good step for her. She'll be interning with an old friend of Mitch Campbell's. It's a *paid* internship."

I was speechless. "Old friend of Mitch Campbell" could only mean one thing. And given my focus of study on economics and political science, that meant they were shipping me to D.C., which was absolutely *not* part of my personal career plans. Aimless, my ass. Just because Linette didn't bother to ask what I wanted to do with my life didn't mean I had no plans to speak of. I couldn't outright refuse, though. The woman was a devious, manipulative bitch who no doubt had my dad on her side already. I hoped that wasn't the case but if I said no out of hand, I'd risk having Dad get involved and I couldn't stand the thought of his disappointment.

Linette gave me a smug look and dabbed a napkin at her lips. "I'll let you absorb everything for a few moments while I visit the ladies room. I'm sure you understand that this is not negotiable. We pulled a lot of strings for you, dear."

She stood and sashayed through the dining room of the restaurant, her designer handbag clutched in her manicured talons and flashes of red from the soles of her expensive pumps taunting me like a matador's cape.

Ben let out a tiny grunt and I realized I'd gripped his hand in mine under the table and now my nails were digging into his flesh instead of my own.

"Calm down, Kat. This can't be all bad."

"This is *worse* than bad, Ben," I hissed. "Who does that fucking bitch think she is? No wonder Dad isn't here. He's probably too fucking embarrassed to have to spring this on me. Fucking coward."

The internship wasn't the issue. I'd already planned to spend my last two semesters interning in Sacramento and staying somewhat close to home while Ben finished his degree. D.C. was technically an improvement, but the fact that Linette had seen fit to orchestrate the move told me she had some ulterior motive in doing so. That's what pissed me off—knowing that was the case, but not knowing precisely what she hoped to gain from it.

Ben tugged his hand free of mine and shifted around in his chair so he could face me at an angle. He withdrew his injured hand from my leg and draped that arm along the back of my chair. A moment later, his other hand slipped back beneath the tablecloth and squeezed my thigh. "We'll figure it out. Call your dad in the morning and see what he can do. In the meantime, I think I know what will help right now."

"A bourbon?"

He smirked at me and shifted his hand a little higher on my thigh. "Something more potent," he said in a low voice, his fingers sliding beneath the hem of my dress.

"Jesus, here? She'll be back any second!"

He just laughed and leaned a little closer. He looked so natural like that. Like we were just having an emotional conversation and he was raptly listening to me. All while his fingertips traced tiny circles up my inner thigh. And oh God did I need him to keep going.

"Mom loves to draw out the torture, you know that as well as I do. I bet I can make you come before she gets back. Even before the waiter brings our food."

I was only slightly skeptical. The boys had gotten me pretty worked up that morning, and in spite of Linette's shit bomb, Ben's touch managed to bring that need back full force. In an attempt to disguise my reaction to him, I leaned an elbow on the table and propped my head on my hand.

"I'll bet you a blow job later that you can't," I countered.

"Sounds good to me, even though I know how much you get off on sucking my cock."

He was right about that—the very thought made my mouth water. I bit my lip and spread my legs a little wider to give him access. "You name the stakes, then," I said, already losing track of reality as his fingertips brushed over the crotch of my panties, then pressed and rubbed through the fabric right against my throbbing clit. I glanced furtively around the restaurant, able to see the entire dining room from the relatively isolated corner table we were seated at. We were beside a high window, but the view from outside was obscured by lush foliage.

"No, I like the sound of that, but only if Andre's at the other end. I love watching him fuck you."

One of the waiters passed by our table and I sat up abruptly and took a sip of my iced tea. My mind raced with the visuals that statement evoked. Now I *really* wanted him to make me come.

I nearly choked on my drink when he pushed the elastic aside and sank his fingers into me. It was an effort to look natural after that point, so I just braced both elbows on the table and leaned my forehead on my palms. Maybe anyone who saw would think I was crying and Ben was just comforting me.

His fingertips slid out of me and stroked up and down the length of my slit, finally stopping at the apex and swirling around and around in tight circles. I *did* cry a little, as a matter of fact, the pleasure of his touch against my clit was so exquisite.

"Oh, God," I breathed, forcing myself to hold still, even though I really wanted to shift my hips to meet the thrust of his fingers when they dipped down and slid back inside me. The thrill of even that little bit of pressure made me squirm in my seat.

"Shhh," he said, dabbing at my cheek with a napkin. "It'll be all right, sis. You'll feel better in a minute, just take a deep breath."

I was already too far gone to smack him for being such an irritatingly cocky jerk, and he seemed to realize it because he sank his fingers in even farther and hooked them to massage that deep part of me that always made me writhe like a crazed woman.

Tears streamed down my face now with the effort of suppressing my reactions to his touch. I let out an inadvertent soft cry and clenched my thighs tight around his hand when he sent me over the edge, holding him trapped there while my orgasm rippled through me. I'd normally have yelled out his or Andre's name, but all I could do was pant and whimper as the spasms clenched at my core, sending waves of tingling pleasure through my entire body. When he finally pulled away, I was a limp mess and needed a tissue for more than one reason.

Linette and the waiter both chose that moment to

reappear. Ben just leaned back in his chair, smug, and gave me a gentle pat on the shoulder.

"Thank you," I whispered. "Jerk." I caught a glimmer of a gratified smile breaking through that asshole façade he liked to wear. Christ, I loved the guy.

At the end of breakfast my mood had descended beyond the point of salvaging. Linette had me against a wall with her plans and threats.

"What the fuck did I ever do to her?" I grumbled to Ben later. We'd left the restaurant on foot—I'd refused to get back in the car with that woman after she'd handed me the paperwork confirming my academic credit transfer for the internship—and found ourselves at an open-air shopping mall staring at movie show times.

I truly felt like crying but Ben's hand on my back helped me keep the welling emotions at bay.

"And what about Andre? Jesus, I can't believe I have to leave in two days!"

"Andre and I will survive," Ben said. "We'll see you at Christmas and maybe find time to come visit, too. It isn't the end of the world, Kat."

I nodded and let him lead me into the theater.

CHAPTER TEN

If anyone had told me a year ago that I'd be in love with two men who were in love with me as well as each other, I'd have laughed. I didn't realize until I was with Ben and Andre how isolated I'd made myself since high school. I'd had few friends during those years, and lost touch with them after graduation. I couldn't call any of my college roommates 'friends'. Even though the girls I'd lived with tried to include me, I had never really been the girly-girl type and didn't quite understand their incessant need for beauty products, fancy clothes, and validation.

Of course if any psychologist dug into my brain, they'd probably tell me I craved attention as much as those girls did, but I sought it out by distancing myself from the mainstream. I wore a lot of black, got tattoos, and fucked a lot of guys, but the most important thing to me was making my classmates kiss my ass by skewing the bell curve. I impressed my professors, but only managed to alienate most of the other students, except for a few of the dimmer bulbs at the opposite end of the curve who were cute and cocky enough to approach me for "tutoring". Dumb guys are so easy to boss around, especially in bed.

Neither Ben nor Andre were dumb, though. Andre had just graduated with honors from the same program I was about to complete the following semester, in spite of his grueling practice schedule. Ben was near the top of his class for pre-law. I'd wondered why I had never run into Andre if he was only a year ahead of me, but I guess star athletes got special treatment. He'd been largely following an independent study track for his last two semesters to work around his game schedule. The man was a machine, which I discovered soon after moving in with him. His level of self discipline astounded me. I think it had a lot to do with the driving need to make his dead father proud by following in his footsteps, but he always managed to find time for me and Ben, too.

So it was a little disconcerting when Ben and I made it home at the end of the day after hours of Ben attempting to cheer me up, and found Andre sitting on the private back balcony, guzzling beer and looking broody. If a man with such a positive outlook and relentless drive as him was sitting there like a lump, then something serious had happened. It made my own little personal drama seem insignificant, even though I still had no idea what was up with him.

Ben and I shared a look, our eyebrows raised in wonder. I kicked off my shoes and slipped through the door to the balcony, padding over to where Andre sat on the comfortable wicker patio sofa, hunched over what looked like his third beer of the evening.

Without saying anything, I stopped in front of him and brushed my hand down the back of his bent head, pausing to squeeze his neck in what I hoped was a comforting gesture. Andre set his bottle down and wrapped both massive arms around my hips, burying his face in my belly. He was shirtless and still carried remnants of his sweet, musky aroma laced with fresh grass that he always had after a long day of practice in spite of having showered.

He sighed and squeezed me tighter. As he leaned back he pulled me with him. I relaxed, folding myself against his strong chest, my backside coming to rest in his lap.

"You wanna talk about it?" I said softly.

Andre just gazed up at me, his soft blue eyes filled with emotions I couldn't even fathom. They were a strange, pale blue I found beautiful and that never ceased to surprise me when he looked at me. He'd had Anglo-Saxon blood on both sides and had somehow ended up with that one recessive gene in spite of a whole slew of contradictory features, not the least of which was the rich, chocolate brown of his skin.

"I love you, Kitty Kat," he said, with such intensity my pulse ratcheted up a few notches. Then he pulled me tighter and kissed me tenderly, his smooth, soft lips embracing my own in their warmth.

Ben had disappeared briefly and now returned, clearing his throat behind us. The kiss had dazed me but I managed to accept the fresh beer he offered before he sat down on the sofa next to Andre.

Andre took both our beers and set them down on the coffee table amid his empties. He reached up to grip the back of Ben's head and pulled my stepbrother into a kiss every bit as slow and sensual as the one he'd just given me. Ben responded with ardor, leaning into Andre. A low moan rumbled deep inside him. When he leaned back again, he looked about as dazed as I felt.

"Andre, you're scaring me," I said. "What the hell is going on?"

"I think I'm leaving," he said. He immediately held up a hand to keep us from spouting the objections and questions Ben and I both had. "Shh. Let me talk. It's not decided one hundred percent yet. Maybe ninety percent."

"Why?" Ben asked, his jaw clenching. He'd been with Andre longer so no doubt he was feeling some harsh feelings right now. If he had the same heavy stone in his belly that I did, I wasn't surprised by his reaction.

"I told you this could happen. My agent brought me an offer from a pro team today. *The* offer."

"So these beers are you celebrating … alone … I take it?" I said with a hint of sarcasm.

"You have to say yes," Ben said, though his tone lacked conviction.

"No, I don't have to do anything. I told the guy I'd sleep on it, but I really just needed to know how you two felt. I have until the morning to give him my answer. If it's yes, then I fly out tomorrow afternoon."

"Of all the days, it had to happen today?" I said. I had to force myself not to think about the ultimatum Linette had thrown at me at the end of breakfast. *Kat, you'll take this internship and be grateful, or I'll tell your father you're whoring yourself out to that foul-mouthed black roommate of yours.* I'd retorted that she didn't know the half of it, but her threat had sunk in. Linette was a master at twisting the truth and Dad had a bad habit of believing everything she said. Now that Andre was dropping another bomb, all the frustration and despair I'd been holding at bay since the morning threatened to escape.

Ben had done his best to try to cheer me up after breakfast. He'd snuck us both into a horror movie, which we sat through twice until my blood rage finally subsided thanks to the vicarious thrills I was watching on the screen. He'd offered to go down on me in the darkened theater but for once I just wasn't interested in sex.

I ruthlessly swiped at the tears spilling from my eyelids, irritated at the realization that my lower lip was quivering.

"Hey, hey. Kat, it's not forever," Andre said. He clasped both hands around my jaw and forced me to look at him. "If I say yes, it'll just be a plane ride. You can come visit. This isn't over, it's just ... on hold until we can figure out a new arrangement."

I shook my head but couldn't speak over the knot that had formed in my throat. When I tried, it just came out as a moan of despair.

"It isn't you," Ben finally offered by way of explanation. "Mom decided to fuck with Kat's life today. She has to take an internship across the country starting Monday. There's really no way for her to get out of it, either. My bitch of a mother made sure of that."

Andre scowled. "Don't talk about your mother that way. I don't care how evil the woman is, she's still your mother."

"She isn't *my* fucking mother, the bitch," I gritted out, but the words broke through the knot and the flood of tears and sobs followed in earnest. I buried my head against Andre's bare shoulder. "I'm losing both of you. And Ben! Ben is, too. We're all going to be alone!"

The weight of that realization hit me like a ton of bricks and I fell apart completely in Andre's arms. He held me tighter while I cried, his large, warm hands rubbing in comforting circles against my back. Ben scooted closer, lending his own comfort with a gentle squeeze of my thigh. The closeness of them now only served to remind me of what I would be missing in only a few days, and I cried harder.

"We'll get through this Kat," Ben said in a quiet, determined tone. "I won't let Mom's schemes get between us, I promise."

"H-how?" I asked, turning my head to peer at him through tear-hazed eyes. I clutched at Andre's shoulders, afraid to let him go now. I knew Ben was right—Andre shouldn't turn down the offer, even for us. But the thought of saying goodbye, even if it was temporary, tormented me.

"I don't know yet, but I'll figure it out. I'm sorry, Kat." He gripped my calves with both hands and lifted them onto his lap so he could move even closer to me and Andre. His hands remained on my lower legs, massaging gently. His face was lined with tension that I realized was his own despair, held in check. We'd have had each other's company with Andre gone, but Linette had managed to ruin that entirely by sending me away, too.

I sniffled against Andre's chest. "It isn't your fault, Ben. I just wish I knew why she's had it out for me my whole life." I sniffled again, irritated by my weak reaction, but the events had been too overwhelming for me to emotionally navigate. I'd never been in love before, even with one man. And here I was about to lose the two who meant the most to me. Tears threatened to burst forth again.

Seeing the waterworks start to spout from my eyes, Ben swiftly pulled off his t-shirt and dabbed at my eyes with it, then my already runny nose. His uncharacteristically chivalrous gesture made me gape at him for a moment.

Ben shrugged at my expression. "Hey, I love you, too. I always hate seeing you cry, you know."

Andre's chest vibrated beneath my ear with a soft laugh. "I didn't think you knew how to cry, Kitty Kat. This is a new one on me."

I looked up at him. "Well get a good look, wise ass. This might be the only time you see me at my worst."

Andre took the wad of soft cotton from Ben and held it to my nose. "Blow, baby."

For a second I was sure "baby" was meant as an insult rather than a term of endearment. I was definitely acting like a baby, but I complied anyway.

Finally mostly dry-eyed and less congested, I glanced at them both. "Better?"

Andre raised a hand and nudged my chin up. He looked at me critically and I could tell from the creases bracketing his mouth that he was making a huge effort to lighten the mood in spite of his own feelings. He nodded once. "Much better," he said, then lowered his mouth to mine.

CHAPTER ELEVEN

My lips tingled under the pressure of his, as if they'd been numbed from my crying and his touch awoke every nerve beneath the surface of my skin. I let out a small moan and relaxed into him, grateful for the contact that helped me forget the ordeal of the day. Emboldened by my reaction, he darted his tongue out, sweeping it between my lips. God, I wanted even more of him—as much as I could get, if this was going to be our last night together for who knew how long.

I wrapped my arms around his neck and met his probing tongue with my own, allowing him access to my mouth and reveling in the sudden penetration of his tongue between my lips.

I'd lost track of Ben for a moment, the comforting warmth of his hands on my ankles all but forgotten in the midst of Andre's kiss. Ben's hands began moving again, sliding slowly up and down my bare shins and calves. The touch that had been merely a comfort a moment ago became more. With each slow stroke he moved his palms higher, sliding up over my knees and then trailing fingertips back down inside my legs with a warm, delicate touch, pushing them apart little by little.

Too absorbed in letting Andre have his way with my mouth, I let Ben do what he would with my lower half. His hands kept sliding higher with each pass, and each time the temperature between my legs grew incrementally hotter.

Andre's body reacted to our kiss with as much apparent desire, the hard, thick rod of his cock pressing against my hip. His hips tilted against my backside and he moaned roughly into my mouth, his lips seeming to lose their grip suddenly. He let his mouth drift across my jaw, trailing urgent kisses as he moved lower. I sighed and tilted my head against his shoulder, letting the soft sweep of his lips on my skin send me into the blissful state I so needed. He paused at my neck to nibble at the sensitive spot beneath my ear before moving on to my collar bone. The man knew just how to distract me from my thoughts. Nothing was left in my mind but pure, raw need for him and for Ben.

I tilted my head to lean against Andre's shoulder, choosing to remain pliant under their combined touch. My emotions were still raw, but becoming less and less prominent compared to the craving I had for their touch.

With his mouth still teasing kisses over my shoulders, Andre slid a hand up my side and cupped one breast. "Christ, I'm going to miss you," he murmured, his touch abruptly growing more urgent. His fingertips tugged at the buttons of my dress, making quick, deft work of them. His hand slid inside beneath my bra, hot against the skin of my breast. He tweaked my nipple into a hard peak, the sharp contact sending a jolt of pleasure southward where it merged with the increasingly arousing sensations of Ben's hands caressing up and down my inner thighs.

Ben shoved my skirt higher up my legs. He urged one leg to bend and pushed my knee wide before bending his head to press his lips against the sensitive skin he'd exposed. His wet tongue made a tickling trail farther up, ending with teasing flicks at the juncture of my hip. The heat between my thighs became a pulsing ember of pure need, urged to burning desire by Andre's teasing touch at my breasts.

Rough hands gripped my hips, fingers hooking into the elastic waist of my panties and tugging. I shifted just enough for Ben to divest me of my panties. Andre got to work on my other garments and soon enough I was gloriously naked in Andre's arms with Ben wasting no time repositioning my legs so he could kneel between them.

Ben's tongue made one long, slow sweep of my

sodden cleft, savoring me and letting out an ecstatic moan as he went. I was immersed in a variety of sensation when Andre dipped his head to capture one nipple between his lips, resuming his caresses of the other with his fingertips.

Andre raised his head, his mouth finding mine again in the middle of my harsh gasps of pleasure. He kissed me roughly and pulled back with a smile.

"You get to come first tonight, Kitty Kat," he said. He threaded his long, dark fingers through Ben's blond hair and pressed my stepbrother harder against my pussy. Ben's tongue sank deep into me in response to Andre's push.

"Damn straight," I managed to gasp before Andre's mouth covered mine again and his tongue invaded. I responded hungrily, clutching at his shoulders. God, how I loved kissing him. Everything about his mouth was delicious, from his full, soft lips to the wet velvet of his tongue sliding against mine. The contact kept me grounded while Ben's tongue between my thighs threatened to send me rocketing into space. I wasn't ready to leave them yet and desperately wanted to make this moment last, but they clearly had other ideas. Andre's free hand slid back up to my breasts, his long fingers easily spanning my chest to tease at both nipples until they ached with tingling pleasure. Soon enough I lost control, Ben's relentless tonguing and finger-fucking of my pussy driving me beyond the edge of pleasure.

I cried out and arched my back, barely aware of Andre's strong arms catching me and holding me while my hips bucked against Ben's mouth. I clutched at Ben's head, holding him tight against me while I rode out the pulsing waves of ecstasy. I went limp as the powerful tremors of my orgasm faded, but didn't release him for a moment. His lips moved and I jerked against him, my flesh oversensitized from his attention. He made a muffled sound, the vibration of it making my pussy quiver, then I realized he was asking if he could stop.

My hands shook when I let them fall away from Ben's head. He sat back on his heels and swiped his hand down over his lips to remove the glistening evidence of my climax.

"C'mere," Andre said gruffly, hooking Ben with one large hand and pulling him into a hard, hungry kiss. Andre sank his tongue into Ben's mouth with such abandon it made my pussy quiver again. He was tasting me on my stepbrother's tongue, and Ben seemed happy to share.

Their needy moans refreshed my addled mind enough to remember my promise to Ben earlier that day. I shifted off Andre's lap and went straight for Ben's belt buckle, tugging it loose and unfastening his jeans in a rush. A second later I had the head of his cock between my lips and both hands circling the length of him.

"Oh, Jesus, yes," Ben muttered. He leaned back and gazed down at me.

I paused long enough to smile up at him. "A bet's a bet, right?"

He just stared at me, dazed. I pressed a hand into the center of his smooth, toned chest and he fell back as I bent and teased my tongue along the underside of his cock, then took him fully into my mouth, letting his cock slide as deep as I could take him.

With my ass aimed at Andre I doubted it would take long for him to take advantage, and I wasn't wrong. I felt him move on the sofa behind me and a second later his dark track pants flew over my head, landing halfway over Ben's enraptured face. His jock strap followed a second later.

"I'm gonna fuck this pretty pussy of yours now, Kitty Kat. You ready for me?"

I "mhmed" around Ben's cock, then drew out the hum as I pulled my lips back along the length of him, sucking just a little harder at his foreskin-covered head. Ben tensed and let out an incoherent moan when I pushed back the skin and slid my tongue around his glistening, pink tip before sinking back down again until the head of his cock pressed against the back of my throat.

"She's so ready for you to fuck her," Ben offered helpfully in a stilted, breathless voice, followed up by, "Oh fuck yeah, Kat. That's so good."

Andre's grip of my hips was the only warning of

his impending entry and he wasted no time. His hot cock brushed up along my slit once before he buried himself hilt-deep, thrusting hard enough to send my mind spinning. I groaned and had to pause sucking Ben until I caught my bearings again and acclimated to the thrusting rhythm of the massive shaft I'd just been impaled with.

Ben's tongue was always a delight to have buried in my snatch. He had a particular knack for knowing exactly what would get me off. Andre had a little less finesse with his cock, but he didn't need it. All he needed to do was show up hard, as far as I was concerned, and I was flying. And when he coupled his relentless thrusting into my pussy with a finger or two circling my tight asshole, then sinking beyond that barrier, it was all I could do not to lose track of what I was doing with my mouth.

Ben chose that moment to hold the sides of my head and thrust up into my mouth with one rough jerk of his hips. He let out a shaky moan as his cum hit the back of my tongue with his salty-sweet flavor. I closed my eyes and held onto him for another moment while I swallowed, then let him slip away. I grabbed the cushion he'd been leaning against and buried my face in it, happy to have nothing else to think about but enjoying the rough penetration of Andre's cock. Soon there was another hand between my thighs, fingertips finding my swollen clit and rubbing in perfect small circles.

They were definitely making up for our interrupted morning fun. I came even harder the second time and relished the primal sounds Andre made as my clenching muscles pulled him over with me. His fingertips dug bruisingly into my hips and I felt his body hunch over mine as his hips thrust with rapid succession and my pussy milked his cock to its limit.

His hot breath hit my shoulder and his hands slid up my sides, arms curling around my torso. He pulled me upright into a tight embrace, his softening cock still buried inside me.

"I love you so much," he said, his voice tight from emotion.

We stayed like that for another moment, still buzzed and coming down from the high of our combined release. Ben flopped back down in front of me, naked and flushed with his beer in one hand. He tilted the bottle back and guzzled it until it was empty.

"Time to drown our sorrows in alcohol now that we're finished drowning them in Kat's snatch," he said, plunking his empty bottle back down on the table amid the others.

Andre released me and I melted into the crook of Ben's outstretched arm, pressing my cheek against his shoulder and curling my legs up onto the sofa. A brown bottle seemed to float into my field of vision, condensation glistening on its surface and the scent of hops wafting from it. I accepted the beer with a grateful smile at Andre and sighed when he sat down on the other side of me, resting a warm hand atop my hip.

"Hey, man, you never told us who signed you," Ben said. "We should probably be drinking champagne now, shouldn't we?"

"Beer's bubbly enough," Andre said. "And don't you think it's a little bittersweet to be celebrating like that? I like this brand of celebration better."

I shifted around so that my back was propped against Ben's side and I could stretch my legs across Andre's lap.

"So, exactly where are we going to be visiting you?" I asked, my stomach flip-flopping at the reminder that he'd be absent after tomorrow. I tamped down the thought of my own departure the day after. Hopefully I'd be able to remain in denial for one more day before it became a reality.

Andre nodded as he swallowed his beer. "Washington," he said, his blue eyes sparkling with pride.

I blinked at him, a sudden surge of hope rushing through me, but I buried it before I could let myself be disappointed if his answer to my next question wasn't the one I desperately wanted.

Cautiously, I said, "Washington … as in Seattle or as in … ?"

"D.C., baby!" he replied with a wide grin.

"Huh," Ben said, as if the detail was only of passing interest.

I sat there with my mouth hanging open trying to

decide if I wanted to punch Andre or kiss him.

Ultimately I gave in to my excitement and launched myself at Andre. I mashed my mouth on his in a sloppy kiss, then yelled at him. "You ass! Why the fuck didn't you say so? Guess where my asshole of a stepmother's sending me?"

Andre's eyes widened as he caught my hint. "Seriously? Oh, baby, you have no idea how happy that makes me."

I threw my arms around his neck, elated at the change in circumstance.

Ben cleared his throat. "Ah … I'm still sitting right here. Love of your lives. Who the two of you are abandoning."

A tiny chill passed through me at his tone. I'd never heard him so melancholy before, and I had the abrupt impression that I'd fucked up somehow, but I had no idea what I'd done wrong. Andre tensed beneath me. We shared a brief glance then looked at Ben.

Ben stood up and gathered his discarded clothes, the scowl on his face plain enough to make my heart hurt as he passed by us and went inside without a backward glance.

CHAPTER TWELVE

When Andre and I ventured inside, Ben was apparently locked in his own room. The room he'd never used during the entire time we'd lived here. I hesitated outside the master bedroom. Every single night for the past six months the three of us had slept in that huge bed together. I'd grown comfortable with the arrangement. Simply knowing there was an attentive man whom I loved dearly to embrace me when I climbed in was enough. Knowing the two of them tended to snuggle as much with each other as they did with me just made it all the more beautiful.

The beauty had dimmed a bit tonight, however. I stood staring at the closed door to the room Ben used for everything but sex and sleep. I'd never seen the door closed before. I started to knock but Andre stopped me.

"Let him be. He'll come around."

I gazed up at Andre, anxious and a little desperate. "Are you sure? When we were kids he could sulk for days."

Andre only shrugged. "I've never fought with him. I have no idea. Go in if you think it will help."

Did Ben need to be alone or was he crying out for attention now? Whatever it was, I wanted desperately to fix it.

I took a chance and knocked.

"Ben? Can we talk?"

No answer. I knocked again.

"Ben, please talk to us."

Still no response. I was on the verge of camping out against the door, but Andre tugged me toward the other room and subdued me with his gentle touch. I buried my face against his chest again, my stomach still tied up in knots. I would be close to Andre during the coming year, which was no small consolation, but I ached for Ben. Over the time we'd been together I'd learned enough about him to know he didn't do well by himself. Our various schedules frequently meant the three of us could be apart for days at a time, only managing to find time together late at night. And when not even a night together was possible, Ben would sink into a dark, sullen mood until we could find time to be together.

"For how long?" I asked, tilting my head up to look at Andre. "How long can he live without us?"

He leaned back and glanced toward the door. "I don't know, but it's killing me."

I eventually fell asleep in spite of my mind churning through all my worries and anxiety over moving so soon. When I woke up Andre was gone and I panicked briefly, worried that he'd left already. My heartbeat finally settled after a moment. He wouldn't have left without saying goodbye, of that I was at least certain.

Voices carried down the hallway and through the cracked bedroom door. They were mostly low, but every so often Ben's strident tone would reach my ears, alternating with Andre's deep, even voice. Ben still sounded upset. I got out of bed and threw on one of Andre's discarded t-shirts, then edged my way down the hallway until I was close enough to hear them without interrupting.

"Don't you dare say you're going to stay for me, Andre. Yes, I hate you both for going. I feel betrayed. Maybe not by you ... by the football league. By my mother. By the fucking universe for all I know. By my own goddamn heart. Just leave already so I can get on with getting over you, all right?"

"Ben..." Andre began.

"Enough! It's bad enough that I have to have this conversation twice. I'm done."

I heard a rustling sound followed by footsteps and then a door slammed. The sound of it reverberated through my body, amping up my anxiety again. I edged my way around the corner to see Andre leaning against the kitchen counter, head bowed and shoulders slumped in defeat. He looked desperate and near tears when he looked up at me.

"I tried," he said, and gave me a weak shrug.

"I know," I said, hesitating to go to him after all the things Ben had said. The truth was, I felt like I was betraying him, too, even though Andre and I didn't exactly have a choice. Neither did Ben, short of sabotaging his college degree. We were all in the same impossible situation. Choosing each other would mean compromising our ideals. Choosing school or career meant compromising our relationship. While I desperately wanted to believe we could survive a year apart, Ben's reaction made me doubt my convictions for the first time.

"You have another day with him," Andre said, a half-hopeful look in his eyes. "Try to get him to come around."

I only nodded.

"I know," Andre said, followed by a rueful chuckle. "He's got it in that gorgeous blond head of his that the world is ending. Not much will talk him out of that idea."

"His world *is* ending. And so is ours." My voice cracked and I struggled to keep the emotions tamped down, otherwise I'd end up a crying mess again.

Andre let out a little strangled sound and abruptly stepped toward me and wrapped me in his arms.

As it was, Ben didn't return that day. I said a tearful goodbye to Andre that afternoon and then focused on packing. The next morning my dad showed up to drive me to the airport. I barely heard anything he said to me, though I sensed some kind of unsaid apology in his words. It just pissed me off more, but I didn't say anything. With Andre now on the other side of the country, I felt split, and I doubted staying in Los Angeles would have helped me or Ben remain whole. The prospect wasn't any more likely once I got to D.C., either.

I was helpless now, and all I could do was simply hope that a year apart wouldn't destroy what the three of us had together.

When I heard Dad say Ben's name, I tore my attention away from the the scenery along the freeway.

"What did you say?"

"Ben's moving home I guess. He said something about your roommate—what was his name?"

"Andre."

"Yeah. Ben said he moved away, too. That's a shame, he seemed like a good guy."

"Did he tell you where Andre moved to?" I asked.

Dad shook his head. We'd reached the airport so I said nothing else until he pulled up to the curb outside the terminal. With all my luggage on a cart, we finally paused and I gave my dad a hug goodbye.

"D.C.," I said as we pulled apart. Dad gave me a quizzical look. "That's where Andre moved to. You can tell Linette. In fact, *please do* tell her exactly that because Ben probably won't and I'd really like her to know." I had a distinctly bitter taste in my mouth remembering my stepmother's threat. Getting the last word only gave me the tiniest bit of satisfaction, however.

Dad's expression clouded. There were so many little things left unsaid between us, but as long as Linette had a hold on him, nothing I said would make it through. He nodded, his face grim as he turned to get back into his car.

"Daddy?" I called just before his head dipped below the car's roof.

"What is it, Katie?"

My heart surged at his old nickname for me. Maybe the sweet guy I remembered from before Mom died and Linette took her place was still in there somewhere. I wished I could figure out how to get him to admit what Linette had done without confessing things I didn't want him to know. There was one thing I could tell him, though.

"Tell Ben I love him."

"I will. Have a safe trip."

Silently I vowed that if we made it through the next year, I'd do whatever it took to keep the three of us together.

PART III
BELONGING

CHAPTER THIRTEEN

Ben plastered on a fake smile for the camera, wishing like hell the day would hurry up and end. His graduation cap itched, and the dark gown had been soaking up the heat of the sun so it felt like a sauna. He should've gone naked underneath like so many of his fellow graduates, but the stunt would've been wasted. The only people who might have appreciated it were all the way across the country.

He hoped he'd be seeing them in only one more day. More than that, he hoped they hadn't entirely forgotten about him. Flying across the country and hunting down Kat and Andre was something he needed to do though. In spite of how they'd left things almost a year ago, he still loved them. He had to find out for himself whether their silence had been due to his own refusal to reach out. He'd been a fool for not trying all year.

Andre had been the only one to reach out to him, though in an indirect way. Ever since his old lover had left to play pro football for a team on the East Coast, Ben had been compelled to watch every single game. It was after one of those games when he'd seen Andre's interview. Prepared for the standard platitudes the players would spout for the camera, Ben had been surprised when his own name spilled from Andre's lips. He didn't remember everything Andre had told the interviewer, but those few words he did remember still echoed in his mind and gave him hope. *"I did it for my dad, of course, but really I owe it all to Kat and Ben."*

His parents hadn't been thrilled with his announcement that he was moving across the country. They expected him to attend law school at Stanford, but he was done being under his mother's thumb. Georgetown was where he had his sights set and it had less to do with the school's merits than its location.

"I'm done with your bullshit, Mom," he bit out, still managing to keep his lips stretched for the sake of the professional photographer.

"Your father and I hoped for more for you, dear. We only want the best," his mother replied, her voice just as stilted as his.

"He's not my dad," he muttered, but said no more because the man in question, Garrett Farrell, was approaching. Ben felt a little guilty for the jab. Garrett had been a better dad to him than the asshole who had left him and his mother for a younger woman when he was ten years old. Garrett also happened to be the father of the woman Ben loved.

Kat's absence still stung. She'd avoided all of them for the past year, not even returning home for the holidays, the animosity between her and his mother like a wound that refused to heal.

"We ready for more photos?" Garrett asked, with jovial humor. The man was no fool, though. Ben's stepdad only affected those mannerisms when he sensed tension between Ben and his mother. Always the diplomat, Kat's father had probably been the biggest reason he and Kat had agreed to attend a local university at the same time. They still hated to disappoint him.

Ben relaxed a bit now that he had another person to divert his attention. Garrett still wasn't entirely an ally — he generally tended to take the side of Ben's mother — but at least he'd never cornered Ben or Kat to assert his agenda.

"I was just trying to impress on Ben the flaw in his plan to move to D.C.," his mother said in her fake cheerful voice.

"He's an adult, Linette. He's made his choice and Georgetown's law program is one of the best. Let him go."

"I'm standing right here, you know," Ben said.

Finally the photographer finished up and handed Ben and his stepdad a card, letting them know where they could order the photographs from. Ben swiftly stripped off his gown and cap, only half aware of what looked like an argument going on between his mother and stepdad a few paces away.

When he glanced at them he was surprised by Garrett's scowl and the angry expression on his mother's face. They'd had arguments before, but nothing that had provoked that kind of a standoff between them in such a public place.

Ben strained to hear what they were fighting about, stepping a couple paces closer. The two of them were too distracted to notice him, and he could just hear their tense voices, pitched low to avoid a scene.

"I know my daughter. Except for your ridiculous plan, she never does anything she doesn't want to do."

"That's my issue. Ben's always been affected by her insane schemes. This is no different."

"Ben's perfectly capable of making his own decisions. If that means being close to Kat, who are we to stand in his way? It's better than them being at each other's throats."

Ben's mother made an exasperated noise. "She's his *sister*. How can you condone such … abhorrent behavior? I did everything I could to make sure that didn't happen and here you are giving your *blessing*?"

Garrett sighed. "They aren't blood siblings. Just because we're married doesn't preclude them from having a relationship."

Ben's mother shook her head. "It isn't only that. It's

been a year. She'll break his heart, I'm sure of it. You know how sensitive he can be."

"Jesus, Linette. Give them a little more credit. I saw them together just before Kat moved. They've never seemed happier."

"Well, that black roommate of theirs is living in the same city as Kat. Did you know that? How do you know she's not *involved* with him now?"

Garrett didn't answer for a second. When he finally spoke again, his voice had acquired a dangerous edge—something Ben had never heard before. "I have never once questioned my daughter's choices or her judgment. I might not agree with everything she does, but I trust her to make the right decision for herself. You could learn a few lessons from her."

With that, the older man stalked off, leaving Ben's mom standing and gaping after him, her mouth working like a fish deprived of water.

Ben was dazed by the revelations of the conversation he'd just overheard. How long had they known about him and Kat? And Jesus, Garrett had been aware of it already and never said a damn thing to him or to Kat. His gut knotted up into a tight, painful ball and heat rose to his face. He stood rooted to the spot, staring in shock at his mother. She had done this to them. *She* had been the mastermind behind making Kat leave, not because of Andre ... because she *knew*. She knew about his and Kat's relationship, and she'd taken Kat away from him.

Slowly, his mother turned, shaking her head as though in impatience. When her gaze fell on Ben, her face paled.

He clenched his teeth and pointed at her. "Don't say another goddamn word, Mother. I'm done with you."

CHAPTER FOURTEEN

Ben spent the next day in a haze of anger and hurt. What would have happened if his mother hadn't manipulated Kat into leaving? Kat wasn't the kind of person to give up easily, but when his mother had played Kat's dad against her, she'd agreed willingly enough. If there was one person in the world Kat hated to disappoint, it was her father. He still remembered seeing the anguish in her eyes their last day together, but he'd been too overwhelmed by his own feelings of loss and abandonment to acknowledge her pain. They'd been quiet that morning while Andre packed and prepared to leave for his cross-country flight. Andre wouldn't let them go with him to the airport. Instead, he'd kissed Ben goodbye and told him to stay—to make sure things were set right between him and Kat again before she had to turn around and leave herself.

Ben hadn't been able to face her, though. He cursed himself now for his ridiculously petulant behavior at the time. He hadn't been able to see past his feelings. All he knew was that she and Andre would be together and that they were leaving him behind.

It wasn't until he was seated on the plane the day after his graduation—almost a full year after that painful farewell—that his emotions shifted toward the positive again. He let out a deep breath when the plane's wheels lifted off the runway, anxious but resolute about his decision. It didn't matter to him how Kat or Andre received him once he found them. As long as they knew the truth. He had felt abandoned and desolate when they left, even though he knew it was beyond their control. He'd known that it was his own mother's doing, but now he knew without a doubt that it hadn't been for the reasons he'd believed.

He managed to sleep through most of the six-hour flight, his dreams drifting like they always did to the last evening spent with the two of them. In it he could taste the sweet tang of Kat's pussy as his tongue slipped between her slick folds. Sometimes the dream would morph into one where he was the only one with her, their skin sliding together as he moved above her, his cock sunk deep inside her hot, hungry channel. Kat always looked so beautiful like that, her dark hair splayed across the pillow and her full breasts bouncing with each of his steady thrusts. Andre would inevitably appear and the pair of them would fuck her again and again, each time drawing more beautiful sounds of pleasure from her lips.

The passenger seated next to him let out a sound of shock that awoke him abruptly, his cock aching and straining at his seatbelt through his jeans. His face heated in shame and he shoved his small pillow into his lap. The elderly lady at his right turned her head toward the window, apparently disgusted.

The erection lingered for longer than he'd have liked, but he couldn't get the dream images out of his mind. Over the past year, he'd had frequent dreams and had always awakened with a gut-wrenching sense of despair over his loss. But his class load coupled with his fear that they'd moved on kept him from contacting them to reconnect. This was the first time since Kat and Andre had left that he awoke feeling pleasantly buzzed from the euphoria of making love with them.

He checked his watch and then stood up from his aisle seat to visit the lavatory before the plane began its descent to the Dulles airport. With his rising anxiety over his reunion with Kat and Andre, his hard-on had subsided. He still maintained a hopeful excitement that had been present ever since he'd walked away from his mother the day before with the understanding that he and Kat didn't need to keep their secret any longer.

His luggage collected, he caught a cab and directed it to Andre's Fredericksburg address he'd tracked down, believing it would be safer to find his old lover first. He was certain Andre would give him a more welcoming reception than he probably deserved. Then perhaps they could see Kat together.

It was close to mid afternoon when the taxi stopped on a tree-lined street in front of a newer-looking brownstone townhouse. His heart pounding hard in his chest, he paid his fare and hauled his heavy suitcases out of the trunk and up the steps. He cursed his shaking hand when he jabbed his finger into the doorbell and waited.

No response.

He leaned to the side to glance through one of the narrow windows that bracketed the wide front door. What if Andre wasn't home? It was late enough in the day, he had hoped Andre might be home but he had no idea what the man's schedule was. It was off-season and training hadn't started, as far as he knew.

He hit the doorbell again and waited, pulling out his phone to flip through his contacts. Andre had sent him a brief text to wish him a happy birthday a few months earlier, but he hadn't responded. He hoped his friend still had the same number.

Just as he hit the "Send" button, the door was flung wide open. Ben's stomach lurched and his head jerked up. Andre's tall, wide-shouldered bulk filled the doorway, his dark chest glistening with water droplets. All he wore was a thick, red terrycloth towel, barely clinging to his hips.

Somewhere inside the townhouse echoed the trill of a cell phone, but Andre didn't seem to hear it.

"Miss me?" Ben said.

"Damn straight," Andre said, his gaze heating as it swept down Ben's body.

Ben almost smiled at Andre's use of one of Kat's favorite phrases, but didn't get the chance. Before he could react, Andre gripped him by the back of the neck and tugged him across the threshold into his arms.

"A fucking year. You should have called me back, asshole," Andre said a second before their mouths crashed together in an urgent tangle of lips and tongues. Nothing else mattered in the moments that followed. Ben immersed himself in Andre's freshly showered scent, breaking their kiss only to bury his face in Andre's neck and inhale deeply.

The door swung shut behind him, and suddenly he was pressed against it with Andre's fingers twining through his hair, tugging his head back. Lips and teeth grazed against his bared throat, kissing and sucking. Ben let his hands roam over the familiar landscape of Andre's body, tracing the lines of all his thick, corded muscles. Ben's cock was rock hard now and he ground his hips against Andre's, their erections aligned perfectly through the layers of fabric that stood as barriers between them.

"This has to go," Ben said, sliding his hands down Andre's stomach and yanking at the towel. The damp length of fabric fell to the floor and Andre's cock was gloriously thick and hot in Ben's palm, twitching under his touch.

Andre groaned and tilted his hips into Ben's stroking palm. "You next," he said in a gruff, urgent voice. His hands tugged at the hem of Ben's shirt, pulling it off over his head. He immediately switched to Ben's jeans, ripping at the buttons and zipper, shoving them and his boxers down over his hips. Andre didn't waste time pulling them all the way off, but pressed his hips in again and gripped their cocks together in his hand.

Ben took hold of them both, too, just above Andre's grip, and they stroked in tandem, each thrusting against each other. He tilted his head back and accepted Andre's mouth against his again, moaning in ecstasy as the friction of their cocks rubbing in their palms sent currents of pleasure through his body.

Andre's tongue swept in hungry licks between Ben's lips, plunging in and surging out again. He nipped and bit as his hips continued their slow grinding against him, his cock hot and soft as velvet in their shared grip. His free hand tangled in Ben's thick hair and tugged his head back. Hot lips descended to Ben's neck and the bites continued, each one reminding Ben how much he had missed Andre's touch and how much he needed to feel consumed utterly and completely by this man. He hadn't forgotten what a joy it was to lose himself with utter abandon to someone he loved.

It didn't matter now. All that mattered was Andre's touch and the rising vibration of their cocks against each other. Andre's balls smacked against his own, their soft weight adding their own sensual caress. He let out a low, long moan, which Andre echoed, sinking his teeth harder into Ben's shoulder. Before he could register them, the waves of pleasure surged through him with violence and his hips bucked up into their hands. Hot streams of semen shot in unison from both tips of their cocks, the bulk of it painting stripes along Ben's stomach.

Ben let his hand fall to his side and released a stuttering sigh. Andre still held them both within his large, gentle grip, his gaze dropping to stare at them in wonder. He stroked them together again.

"I missed this," he said. His gaze met Ben's, but something in his eyes seemed distinctly sad.

Without having to ask, Ben understood that look. In spite of the amazing reunion, something was still missing.

"You haven't seen her, have you?" Ben asked.

Andre expelled a deep breath and handed Ben his discarded towel. "Not for months. We lost touch after the season started. I tried, but she stopped answering my calls and texts."

"Are you busy tonight?"

"Only with you," Andre said.

CHAPTER FIFTEEN

Ben only took enough time to shower and try to shake off some of the travel weariness before the pair of them hopped into Andre's car to head to Georgetown where Kat lived.

"You should have called," Andre said.

Ben nodded, letting his eyes fix in the distance on the darkening sky and the rising moon.

"I've made a lot of mistakes. But I'm here now, so hopefully that counts for something."

"Well, like I said, I haven't seen her in months, but I have friends who know her. I don't know if we're going to like what we find."

Ben's stomach twisted. "What do you mean?"

"I mean it sounds like she's been in a dark place for a long time. You know her, man. She wouldn't even talk to me, and trust me, I tried. I even went to her place once around Christmas, but she wouldn't open the door. So I just left her present in the hallway."

"Maybe she'll let us in when she finds out what I have to tell her."

Andre glanced at him then turned back to the road. "It better be good to get her to come out of her shell again."

"It has to do with our parents."

"You mean like something tragic?"

"Depends on your perspective. Losing each other was pretty tragic. But no, not tragic — nobody's dead, anyway."

Andre relaxed a bit. "That's good."

"Yeah, but they've apparently known about us all along, or at least for awhile. It wasn't you my mother hated the idea of Kat being with. She was trying to drive me and Kat apart. And it fucking worked."

"Fuck, seriously? What about her dad?"

"Well, the bastard didn't try to stop my mom so he doesn't earn any respect from me for that, but I think he might have come around just before I left. Not that it matters now, though. The damage is done."

"It means a lot that you came. To me, I mean. With any luck seeing the two of us will turn her around."

"You still love her, too."

"Always. You guys are what make me whole. I had my team to distract me this past year, but I'm still a rookie to them. None of them know anything about my life, outside the game anyway, and they'd never replace the two of you. I want you back. Both of you."

They pulled into a small parking lot of an older building in Georgetown with well-kept landscaping decorating the exterior. If everything went well with Kat, maybe Ben would be living here soon too. He had to remain optimistic, because he couldn't imagine any other outcome at this stage. The prospect of having to endure another second of his life without both her and Andre in it threatened to sink him into the darkness that he'd barely managed to keep at bay over the past year. Andre had had football to keep him sane. Ben had been distracted by his drive to finish his degree, refusing to spend precious energy on anything but that goal. He hoped Kat had found something to help her stay sane through it all, but if Andre's assessment told him anything it was that Kat had fared far worse than either of them.

And it was his fault.

They snuck through the front door as another tenant exited and made their way up the wide staircase. The apartment building itself was well lit and brightly decorated, in spite of its age, but Ben barely noticed the decor. The closer they got to Kat's door, the more he dreaded what they would find when they got to her.

6B. The number loomed in front of him and Ben stood paralyzed. Finally Andre reached past him and knocked.

Ben thought he heard music emanating through the door, and voices. Andre knocked again, and a second later the music quieted. The door rattled as the locks were disengaged and his heart lurched as it swung inward.

"Well, fuck me," Kat said.

Ben struggled to even give her a weak smile, as surprised as he was by the sight that greeted him. She was a mess, true enough. Her dark hair was sticking out in every direction, teased up from sleep, which seemed odd considering the lateness of the day. And she was dressed only in a rumpled blue and white striped chambray shirt. A man's shirt, he observed abstractly. In fact, now that he gave her another once-over, she had the appearance of that perfect sexy mess that he loved, a look she only had right after being thoroughly fucked.

"I suppose you want to come in, huh, stepbrother mine? Hey, Andre," she added almost as an afterthought. "You're a little late, so don't mind the mess, or the man."

Mess was an understatement. Her place was littered with clutter, barely a square foot of floor was visible beneath clothes and magazines and general detritus. Oddly enough her kitchen was spotless.

And there was a half-dressed man lounging on the sofa.

Ben and Andre made their way carefully into the living room and managed to find a somewhat clear space of floor where they could stand near her fireplace.

"It's good to see you Kitty Kat," Andre said. Ben caught him looking pointedly at the man on the sofa. "You plan on introducing us to your friend?"

Kat made a dismissive noise and flapped her hand as she headed to the fridge. "That's just Derek."

Derek snorted and stood. He reached out a hand to Andre. "Derek Campbell. She's not the most hospitable person this time of day, sorry for that."

Andre shook the man's hand, his knuckles turning pale with the pressure he exerted. "Andre Kingston," he said in a distinctly menacing voice.

Ben was sure he heard Derek's bones cracking within Andre's grip.

Derek's face went pale, his eyes filled with both surprise and pain. He glanced at Ben for a moment, his expression almost plaintive. Andre finally released him and Derek shook his hand, flexing his fingers and wincing.

"Wow, ah … that's quite a grip. I should've recognized you, sorry for that. I don't suppose I could get your autograph?"

Andre just stared at Derek until the man wilted and sank back down onto the sofa muttering something that sounded like, "nevermind, forget I asked." Ben knew exactly how withering those blue eyes could be when Andre got it into his head to be pissed, which was rare.

Kat trotted back into the room, her lithe gait hopping gracefully over the mess, and handed them each a fresh beer. She hauled an armload of what looked like half-folded laundry off an armchair and disappeared with it. "Have a seat," she said when she came back, pushing Ben toward the chair.

He hated the utter lack of emotion in her reactions, and hated even worse the cocky look on Derek's face.

"How do you know my sister?" Ben asked, leaning his elbows on his knees and clutching his beer.

"Through work. We're both interns for Congressman Greeby, thanks to my dad. I didn't know she had a brother."

The name finally registered. Campbell. The Campbells were old family friends, but Ben hadn't seen Derek since the two were kids. He hadn't particularly liked him then, either.

"Stepbrother, actually," he said, thinking how much he'd really like to punch Derek and throw him out the window.

"Right, that's cool. So what was it like growing up with our little spitfire here? She's something else, isn't she?"

"You have no idea," Ben said, gritting his teeth and taking a long swig of beer.

"No seriously, I'd love to hear some stories."

Ben glanced past Derek to Kat, who had taken up a spot on a barstool a few feet behind Derek, watching the proceedings with a demented sort of glee. Her eyes were slightly glazed from alcohol, but she seemed to be having the time of her life. He was reminded of Christmases when they were younger. He'd always dreaded opening gifts from Kat, but their parents made him do it anyway. Kat had gotten off on seeing him squirm, but she'd never known how much he secretly loved the gifts even though they embarrassed him to have to open in mixed company.

"Oh yeah? Here's a story," Ben began, keeping his eyes on Kat's. "Once upon a time there was a little girl named Kat who thought she'd torture her stepbrother by fucking a loser. Little did she know that her stepbrother realized it was just a cry for attention, and so he and his friend beat the loser to a bloody pulp and threw him out the window. She never fucked another loser after that. In fact, she appreciated what her stepbrother had done so much she promised she'd get her shit together and behave like a human being again."

"What the fuck?" Derek asked, but Ben ignored him, too smug over Kat's reaction to give a crap about the idiot on the sofa.

Kat's expression had soured. "Did you ever think that maybe Kat wouldn't have been fucking losers to begin with if her asshole of a stepbrother had been around to talk to all along?"

"Andre was here, Kat."

"But you weren't. You weren't fucking available to me. I needed you both. All or nothing—do you know what that means?"

Andre's deep voice cut in. "We're with you now, Kitty Kat. It's been that kind of year for us, too."

"Except we weren't fucking losers." Ben said.

Kat rolled her eyes and looked pointedly at Andre. "You haven't been around for the local tabloid drama, Ben. Andre, why don't you tell him what you've really been up to in your free time? Getting caught in compromising positions with senators' daughters? No, Ben. We've been surviving the only way we know how. Being with Andre just hurt too much without you there, too. And believe me, we did try."

Ben turned to stare at Andre, who just shrugged and gave him a sad little smile. "She ain't lying. It's been a rough year."

"So, let me get this straight," Derek said, his eyes wide and his mouth opened in a giddy, stupid grin. "You've been fucking both these guys—one is your own stepbrother and the other's the newest addition to the Redskins? Wow, you really are a dirty little whore, aren't you?"

Ben didn't even register his own movements to get to the guy. Before Derek could expel the laugh that was rising in his chest, Ben's fist smacked into his nose with a satisfying crunch. He was gratified when Andre's large hand clamped down on the back of Derek's neck and hauled him toward the door like he weighed nothing.

"What the fuck!" Derek bellowed.

"Oh, you'd rather I actually throw you out the

window?" Andre offered, altering his direction slightly toward the window.

"No! No! Just let me the fuck go!"

Andre made it to the door and tossed Derek out, shirtless. "You breathe a word of this to anyone, I'll find you, you worthless piece of shit."

CHAPTER SIXTEEN

When the reverberation of the slamming door finally subsided, Ben glanced at Kat and flexed his bruised fist.

"You got any ice? That fucker had a hard head."

Kat sighed and sauntered around the bar into the kitchen. The shirt she wore just covered the tops of her thighs and it rode up, displaying the lush curve of her bottom when she reached into the freezer and rummaged around.

Ben wandered closer, fascinated by a tendril of ink that peeked out, curling down over the back of her hip and lower, like the sinister leg of a dark spider. When he was close enough, he reached out a hand and gently lifted the edge of the shirt to see.

Kat froze in place, frost-rimed air billowing out of the freezer around her while Ben's fingertip traced the deep black pattern of the tattoo that graced the curve at the top of her right buttock and curled around and down over her hip. The design was a stylized trio of letters, merged together in a triangle. Their initials — B, K, and A — their ligatures long and curling, entwined with each other around a tiny red heart.

"It was the only way I could keep you two close," she said. She pulled a bag of frozen peas out and leaned back to shut the door. Her movement pressed her backside into his palm and he let his hand slip lower, his fingers alive with the electric sensation of her smooth, hot skin.

"We're here now," Ben said.

She turned without pulling away from him and gripped his right hand, pressing the frozen bag against his knuckles.

"Why didn't you at least call, Ben? Just once?" She stared up at him, her eyes wide and full of hurt. He'd caused that, and now he had to atone. But how?

"I was too angry for a long time. Not exactly my wisest period, I admit. And by the time it occurred to me what an ass I'd been, it was too late. Tell me, Kat, would you have answered if I'd called you in September?"

She lowered her gaze and squeezed his fingers where they still rested in her hand. "No, probably not. I'd already started my crazy bender of booze and hot men by then. I was too humiliated by my own bullshit to talk to anyone who cared about me for a long time. I still am, a little bit, but you're here, so …"

He was baffled by the change in her. The cocky, irreverent Kat he remembered seemed chastened now.

"I never wanted to do this to you, Kat. I'm so sorry."

"Anyway, I would understand if you don't want me anymore. Hell, I can't even stand myself most days."

"Jesus, no," he said, gripping her fingers and dislodging the frozen vegetables from the top of his hand. "I've never stopped loving you, not for a second since we were twelve." He tugged her closer and wrapped both arms tightly around her, burying his face in her tangled curls. Christ, she smelled amazing. Her soft curves pressed against his torso as she sank into him like she'd never left.

She moaned into his throat when he slid his hands down her back and gripped her bare ass beneath the shirt. He turned and pressed her back against the fridge, tilting his head down to find her lips. She opened up eagerly, letting his tongue slide between her lips and greeting it with tentative touches of her own. Her fingers threaded into his hair and clawed lightly at his scalp and neck.

He couldn't help but touch her everywhere. He'd dreamed about her so many times over the past year, but as vivid as the dreams had been, they paled in comparison to her flesh. The salty-sweet flavor of her skin delighted his tastebuds and her nipples tightened just like he remembered when his hand reached under her shirt and found her breast. He tugged the shirt aside and bent to tease one dark pink tip with his mouth, eliciting a lovely sigh.

Working his way lower, he unfastened the last few buttons of her shirt and slid down her body, landing on his knees with his mouth pressed against her navel.

Before he could slide his palms up to the apex of her thighs, she clamped her legs together and pushed him away.

"Stop. Don't do that, please."

He blinked up at her, then down at his target. She'd apparently given up on regular trims, but that didn't bother him a bit. He just wanted her.

"What is it? I don't care about this if that's what you're worried about," he said, rubbing his fingers lightly through the dark triangle of curls between her thighs that he knew concealed an elaborate tattoo.

"Not that. Let me shower first, all right? And actually, as much as I'd love to get down and dirty right away, I really, really need to get the fuck out of this pigsty for awhile."

"It's because you were with him today, isn't it?" Ben asked, standing up and caging her between his arms so she couldn't move. "You're embarrassed, aren't you? Because you fucked that loser Campbell. Let me guess. You didn't enjoy it, did you?"

She laughed. "He's got about as much finesse in the bedroom as a gorilla. You guys never gave me bed hair this bad." She pointed at the tangled mess that crowned her scalp.

He smiled and glanced at Andre who rested patiently in the armchair, watching them intently. He rose in response to Ben's unspoken message. Both men were good at reading each other, particularly when it came to what they planned to do with Kat.

"Fine, then I won't go down on you yet …" he began in a low voice, "but I think you need a reminder of what you've been missing before I let you out of my sight again, even for five minutes."

He tugged her shirt wide open again and cupped her left breast, tracing the shape of the dragon tattoo that curved around the outside of her creamy flesh with his fingertips. Bending his head again, he took her nipple in his mouth and sucked hard.

Out of the corner of his eye, Andre loomed, his shoulder brushing against Ben's as he moved in close and bent to kiss Kat. His dark hand cupped her other breast while their mouths tangled, then his face moved down alongside Ben's to capture her other nipple between his full lips.

Ben heard a thump and a moan as Kat flung her head back against the fridge door.

He and Andre had the same thought, their hands sliding down her stomach and bumping against each other as they aimed for her pussy. Ben let his hand rest on her upper thigh, caressing her lightly while Andre delved deeper, teasing his fingers back and forth between her legs.

"So wet," Andre murmured. "Need to fuck this

sweet pussy. Missed you so much, Kitty Kat." His voice was urgent and only semi coherent between his licking and sucking of her torso. At first his aim seemed off, wandering over her in erratic sweeps, until he simply collapsed to his knees and pulled her down to him.

Ben stood back and let her go. She collapsed into Andre's arms, succumbing to his touch. He shoved the shirt off her shoulders to get at more of her skin, then laid her down on the pristine tiles of the floor. Before Andre could move closer, Ben clutched him by the shoulder and tugged at the hem of his shirt.

Without a word, Andre stripped off his shirt and let Ben help him out of his shoes and jeans. Kat surged up on her knees and pulled at the waistband of Andre's boxers, pausing to stroke his cock once before he was fully naked. Nothing but hot urgency showed in Andre's gaze when he grabbed Ben's head and kissed him deeply, then hurriedly helped Ben shed his own clothes. They sank down on either side of Kat, pulling her to the floor and taking her breasts in their mouths again. This time Andre tugged Ben's hand down between Kat's thighs and she sighed when his fingers found her slick clit and stroked her.

"God, I need you both right now. Please, please fuck me." Kat clutched at Ben, rolling onto her side. She slung a thigh across his hips, pushing him onto his back, and rose above him, her glorious breasts jiggling alluringly when she leaned down to kiss him. She reached between her thighs and wrapped her hand around his cock, the lightest slide of her fingers along his length making him twitch against her.

She held him tightly, pressing his tip against her swollen clit and swirling it around in a circle until her flushed cheeks grew redder from her arousal and her eyelids fluttered with ecstasy.

"Let me inside you, baby," he said, aching from her teasing.

Andre's hands came around her from behind, cupping her breasts while his knees came to rest on either side of Ben's thighs.

"Let him in that tight little snatch of yours, Kitty Kat. He's missed you as much as I have."

Kat smiled and tilted her head back against Andre's shoulder. "Oh? And where will you be?"

"Right back here," he said, letting one hand slip down her side and behind her. A second later the hand reached through her thighs and took over stroking Ben's cock, rubbing its tip with maddening slowness against Kat's clit some more. Finally Andre aimed him just so and Ben felt the slick heat of Kat's opening engulf the throbbing head of his cock and tighten.

"Oh, God," she exclaimed, opening her eyes to look at him. She leaned over, bracing her hands on his chest, and kissed him while he lifted his hips, letting himself experience the delicious, velvet warmth of her by slow increments. Blood pounded in his ears as much as in his cock, the sheer pleasure of her hot sheath sending his pulse skyrocketing.

She let out a rough moan against his lips and pulled back slightly. He caught a glimpse of Andre, his thick chest rising and falling, one hand clutching Kat's hip tightly while the other teased between her ass cheeks. Andre's blue gaze darted up once and rested on Ben, then he glanced around the kitchen. He had to lean only a short way to reach onto the counter and snag a clear bottle with pale golden liquid inside it.

Ben's vision faltered amid the increased tempo of Kat's fucking, but he managed to see the label just before Andre upended the bottle above the cleft of Kat's ass. "Olive Oil," it read upside-down as the pale, clear liquid drizzled out of a long, narrow steel spout. Give the man props for resourcefulness.

He closed his eyes then, holding Kat closer so he could keep her mouth against his. He never wanted to let her go again as long as he lived. Right now, however, they all just needed to fuck each other into oblivion.

Kat's moans became more urgent as Ben felt the pressure on his cock increase. She froze in place with his cock held halfway inside her.

"Relax, Kitty Kat." Andre's deep voice resonated. Kat let out a sigh and leaned farther down to sink her fingernails into Ben's shoulders.

"Don't stop!" she called behind her. She looked

back down at Ben, her eyes wet from tears and her mouth half open in ecstasy.

Ben slid his hand into the tight space between them, reaching between her thighs until he found her clit, swollen and throbbing and still slick from her arousal. She let out a harsh whimper when he pressed his fingers tight against her and began to rub.

"That's right, baby," Ben said. "Relax and let him in. I can feel his cock sliding into your tight ass. You like that, don't you? Having us both filling you up like this?"

She only managed to murmur a couple syllables that sounded like "mhm" before her eyes closed and she emitted a harsh groan.

At the same moment Andre's cock slid deep into her, its thick length pressing Ben's cock hard against Kat's pelvis. When Andre slid back out and thrust in again, Ben nearly lost his mind. He rubbed frantically at Kat's clit, struggling to maintain his own rhythm as he thrust his cock back into her.

Kat's lips slid against his, moving slightly, her throat forming some semblance of speech, but Ben couldn't make out the words. Perhaps it was only his own mind that had lost its ability to comprehend language anymore, or perhaps being filled by two cocks made it impossible for her to speak.

He wasn't even sure who came first. It might have been Kat, her clenching muscles tightening like a vise around his length as he fucked deep into her. Her tiny clit was the first sign, however, the bundle of nerves quivered and pulsed under his fingertips, and from there they came like a tumbling line of dominoes.

Ben's cock exploded within her and he cursed incoherently. Kat fell on top of him, gasping, and Andre's thick cock slammed deep into her ass, the stiff rod of flesh jerking with his climax.

Andre's hands smacked down on the tiles on either side of Ben's head. The man's blue eyes peered at Ben across Kat's shaking shoulder. A soft sob hit their ears and Andre's brow creased. He lifted one hand and gently rested it on Kat's shoulder.

"Hey, girl, are you okay? I didn't hurt you, did I?"

Kat shook her head. "No. Jesus you guys, I never thought I'd get to feel this alive again. Never leave me again, okay?"

"Not on your life," Andre said.

"If you promise to stay, so will I," Ben added.

Kat laughed. "You've got a deal."

CHAPTER SEVENTEEN

It had to be the craziest scheme Ben had concocted in his entire life, rivaling some of the pranks he'd pulled on Kat when they were kids. He couldn't imagine the two of them would say no—at least not with the speech he had in mind.

The plan had taken him a week to work out once he'd made the decision to go through with it. But he intended to do it right, so he went all out. The easy part was getting the money without asking Andre. He still had access to the rainy day fund he and Kat had saved while living with Andre after they'd first gotten together, so he dipped into that, just about cleaning it out. Money mattered less to the three of them than staying together, so he felt little guilt over spending such a sum on his plan. The two of them were worth it.

The expensive restaurant was easy, too, along

with the few palms he had to grease to ensure everything went smoothly once the three of them were there.

The tricky part was coming up with a ruse to get them dressed up and agree they deserved a night out together. Ultimately he relied on Andre for that. It was Kat's birthday, and the first time the three of them would be together for a birthday of theirs.

Andre had started asking Ben for gift ideas weeks earlier, but Ben brushed him off with the excuse that his gifts for Kat over the years had usually been for the purpose of revenge. Eventually, he dropped the hint that Kat might like to really celebrate with a fancy dinner like her dad used to have for her when she was younger. Planting that small seed was all he needed to do, along with offering to handle the reservations in Andre's name if Andre handled the bill and agreed to take care of surprising Kat.

The night couldn't be going any better if he'd tried, either. Kat looked dazzling in a slinky silver cocktail dress, her dark curls sweeping over her pale, bare shoulders. He and Andre were both in designer suits, which Andre had insisted on paying for. Ben was grateful for that, since he'd spent just about all he had available already.

They were all a little tipsy from their drinks. Kat and Andre were the happiest he'd seen them since they'd moved back in together at the beginning of the summer. The last few months had been the happiest of

Ben's life, too. There was just one more thing he had to do to make sure it stuck this time.

His heart pounded as he made the subtle signal to their waiter. He scooted a little closer to Kat, pressing his lips lightly against her shoulder to try to calm himself enough to get the words out that needed to be said.

Her laugh tickled his eardrums as she cupped his chin and kissed him back. "This is the best birthday ever," she said, smiling brightly.

"It's not over yet," he said.

The waiter arrived as though on cue, setting down three bubbling flutes of champagne and leaving the bottle in a bucket at the edge of their private booth.

Kat was too giddy to notice, but Andre's sharp gaze rarely missed a thing. His blue eyes widened when he picked up his champagne, his brows raised in a question.

Ben quirked his lips and squeezed Kat's thigh to silence her.

"There's something I need to tell you guys," he said in a serious tone.

Kat's expression clouded. Her gaze remained fixed on him while she toyed with the stem of her glass, still unaware of what was transpiring.

"You'd better not be leaving," she said.

"Nothing like that. The last few months have been a dream come true for me after being apart. All my fault, of course."

"I disagree," Kat said. "All *Linette's* fault. I stopped blaming you months ago, Ben."

"Fine, but I think we all agree that we don't want something like that to happen again, right?"

He paused, trying to remember all the words he'd so painstakingly rehearsed over the last week, but they'd deserted him entirely. The moment was upon him now.

And they were looking at him, expectant. Andre's smile widened as he caught on, but Kat only looked at him like he'd just said the most obvious thing in the world.

"Ah, Christ, you guys. I think we should get married. Be careful drinking your champagne, Kat."

Kat's mouth dropped open in shock and she finally looked at her glass. She held it up to the light. "Holy shit, Ben. Boy does this ever make up for all those lumps of coal you put in my Christmas stocking when we were kids."

She tilted the glass back and swallowed its contents, until the ring clinked against the rim and she caught it neatly between her teeth.

"What about Andre?" she asked.

Andre raised his own glass in a silent toast to Ben and tossed it back. Ben was worried he'd actually swallowed the ring, when Andre grinned and opened his mouth, the large, shining band hooked on the end of his tongue. He plucked it off and slid it onto his finger.

"That's a 'yes', in case you were wondering," Andre said. "But I think you've forgotten a key detail regarding legality here. You might get yourself kicked out of law school if you're not careful, babe."

Ben waved a hand. "Not worried about that. I just want you guys to have no doubts about my commitment in this. I think the two of you *should* make it legal at some point, but these rings are my way for all three of us to have a constant reminder of that commitment. Like you said when I first got to D.C, Andre—you two make me whole. I'm never giving that up again."

He swallowed his own drink and fished out his ring, a perfect match to theirs. The jeweler had crafted the rings from layers of three different metals, the swirls of the pattern mesmerizing to him in the candlelight. He'd tell them the story of commissioning the rings later. Tonight, he just needed to be with them.

Kat stared down at her ring with a frown. "This is nice, Ben, but I won't say yes until you do something for me. Both of you, actually."

"Anything," he and Andre said simultaneously.

"If you're going to make a commitment, it needs to be more permanent. Matching tattoos should do it. And I get to choose where they go."

"Put that ring on and you have a deal," Ben said.

"Gladly." Kat grinned at him, and a bubble of laughter rose up in her chest. She threw her head back and nearly howled with mirth over something.

Ben and Andre both stared at her like she'd gone nuts.

"Oh, your mother is going to *hate* this!"

Thank you for reading "Blackmailing Benjamin"! If you loved it, please visit the retailer and leave a review!

And don't forget, subscribing to Ophelia's Dragon Beasties mailing list gets you **two free sexy dragon shifter stories** not available for sale anywhere and gives you direct access to updates on future stories by Ophelia.

Casey's Secrets

She could taste the sting.

Casey's always had desires that set her apart, even from her best friend. The moment she turned eighteen she decided to take control of her life and explore those darker fantasies. Now that she's a fresh high-school graduate, she's looking forward to her first summer as an adult and having the freedom to finally take control of her life and find out what these cravings of hers really mean. But one slip and a missed curfew might screw up her entire summer.

Max has been Casey's hero for years, ever since marrying Casey's mother. His only flaw is how rigid he is about the rules as long as Casey still lives at home. After her little misstep, he won't let her off lightly. She must choose between being grounded for the summer, or enduring a single spanking that will free her to enjoy her vacation.

Casey makes her choice, but neither she nor Max are prepared for the domino effect a few smacks to her backside will have, or the secrets that will be revealed as a result.

Both of them have something to hide, but they might have more in common than they realized.

Buy Now.

Burying His Desires

Some things fit together better after they're broken.

A 3AM call is never good news, and for eighteen-year-old Britannia Vale, it's the worst. The man who raised her is on the other end, relaying a tragedy that will tear her entire world apart.

In the midst of grief, Britannia and Michael struggle

to pick up the pieces, but the old pieces don't quite fit together they way they used to. She's no longer the little girl Michael helped her mother raise. Michael is still her hero, but looks at her in a way that incites overwhelming desires for the only man who can keep her whole in the aftermath of her mother's death. What's worse is that she might be the only person who can keep him whole, too.

How far will Britannia and Michael go to put the pieces back together?

Buy Now.

ABOUT OPHELIA BELL

Ophelia Bell loves a good bad-boy and especially strong women in her stories. Women who aren't apologetic about enjoying sex and bad boys who don't mind being with a woman who's in charge, at least on the surface, because pretty much anything goes in the bedroom.

Ophelia grew up on a rural farm in North Carolina and now lives in Los Angeles with her own tattooed bad-boy husband and six attention-whoring cats.

Subscribe to Ophelia's newsletter to get updates directly in your inbox. If newsletters aren't your thing, you can find her on social media.

http://opheliabell.com/subscribe

facebook.com/OpheliaDragons
twitter.com/OpheliaDragons

ALSO BY OPHELIA BELL

Sleeping Dragons Series

Animus

Tabula Rasa

Gemini

Shadows

Nexus

Ascend

Sleeping Dragons Omnibus

Rising Dragons Series

Night Fire

Breath of Destiny

Breath of Memory

Breath of Innocence

Breath of Desire

Breath of Love

Breath of Flame and Shadow

Breath of Fate

Sisters of Flame

Rising Dragons Omnibus

Dragon's Melody (a standalone dragon novel)

Immortal Dragons Series

Dragon Betrayed

Dragon Blues

Dragon Void

Dragon Splendor

Dragon Rebel

Dragon Guardian

Dragon Blessed

Dragon Equinox

Dragon Avenged

Immortal Dragons Box Sets:

Immortal Dragons: Books 1, 2, & 3 + Prequel

Immortal Dragons: Books 4-6 + Epilogue

Black Mountain Bears

Clawed

Bitten

Nailed

Stonetree Trilogy

Fate's Fools Series

Deva's Song (Fate's Fools Prequel)

Fate's Fools

Fool's Folly

Fool's Paradise

Fool's Errand

Nobody's Fool

Eye of the Hurricane

Fool's Bargain

April's Fools

Thieves of Fate

Aurora Champions Series

(Set in Milly Taiden's "Paranormal Dating Agency" world)

The Way to a Bear's Heart

Hot Wings

Triple Talons

Midnight Star

Once in a Dragon Moon

Rebel Lust Erotica

Casey's Secrets

Blackmailing Benjamin

Burying His Desires

Standalone Erotic Tales

After You

Out of the Cold

Printed in Great Britain
by Amazon